LOVE IN MOTION

LOVE IN MOTION

•

Theresa Goldstrand

AVALON BOOKS
THOMAS BOUREGY AND COMPANY, INC.
401 LAFAYETTE STREET
NEW YORK, NEW YORK 10003

© Copyright 1998 by Theresa Goldstrand
Library of Congress Catalog Card Number 97-97115
ISBN 0-8034-9276-6

FIRST PRINTING

PRINTED IN THE UNITED STATES OF AMERICA
ON ACID-FREE PAPER
BY HADDON CRAFTSMEN, BLOOMSBURG, PENNSYLVANIA

To Dale, the auburn-haired Viking
who shares my days and my dreams

Chapter One

He heard the car before he saw it. The low hum of a finely tuned engine droned in the distance before a low-slung sports car topped the hill at Jaw Bone Canyon. Jann Erikson trained his gaze on the flashy cocoa-brown Jaguar XKE and zeroed in on the long-haired blond behind the wheel.

"Where do you suppose she's going?" the young gas jockey asked, as he returned the gasoline hose to its holder.

Jann watched as she disappeared into the canyon. "Not far, I'd bet."

"What d'ya mean?"

Jann handed a ten-dollar bill to the attendant and slid his wallet into the back pocket of his jeans.

"Smell that?" He inhaled deeply and caught the faint smell of antifreeze that carried on the warm desert air. "She'll be down before she hits the 395 intersection. Mark my words."

1

The young man shook his head.

"And I'll be right there to help her out." Jann laughed and climbed into his vintage tow truck. "See ya later, Joey."

"Take it easy, Jann."

"Got to. Top speed is thirty-five in this old heap."

Tracey tightened her grip on the smooth wooden steering wheel as she entered the mouth of Red Rock Canyon. Her eyes strayed to the gleaming brass dash plaque that read: *Tracey Evans, 1996 participant—Soda Springs Rally*, just before towering canyon walls blocked the sun and blanketed the sleek Jaguar in shadows.

The powerful engine growled like an unleashed animal as she downshifted to begin maneuvering the winding curves. Sheer cliffs bordering either side of the highway not only effectively hid travelers from the harsh sunlight, but provided a cool respite from the barren Mojave Desert.

She rolled her window down and inhaled deeply. It was a cool wind that swept past her face and coaxed long strands of hair loose from the ribbon at the side of her neck. She accelerated as she pulled out of the curve and headed into yet another.

The canyon opened into a sandy draw and the glaring sun once again burst through, momentarily blinding her. She goaded the car into the next bend, pushing it as hard as she dared. The speedometer climbed to well above the speed limit. She backed off the accelerator and shoved the clutch in at precisely the same moment when she threw it into third.

Tracey tromped the gas pedal when she entered the long, sweeping curve. This curve didn't reverse direction as the others had, but continued in a semicircle around an ancient lava mound. She felt the back tires lose traction and the sleek-bodied machine begin to fishtail. Lifting her foot from the accelerator, Tracey's forearms stiffened as she tried to control the slide.

"Back off, back off," she whispered.

The tires grabbed the road and straightened out. She expelled her breath in a noisy whoosh and felt her heart pound in her chest. Beads of perspiration gathered on her brow as she left the coolness of the canyon and bolted onto the ridge heading north. It was a long straight stretch in front of her as far as she could see.

Her heart slowed its rapid beating as she took time to wipe her sweaty palm on her jeans. She eyed the large stopwatch taped to the dash, then cheered. "All right! One minute twenty-five seconds—two miles—not bad."

A quick glance in her rearview mirror revealed an empty highway. The air that tore past now couldn't have been the same as that in the canyon. It was dry and hot and scraped the moisture from her face. In anticipation of the heat, she had applied a generous amount of lip gloss before she left Santa Monica. She pressed her lips together, and rolled the window up again to block the hot wind.

"How anyone could live in this godforsaken desert is beyond me," she muttered. "Give me the beaches, the fog, the ocean . . ."

As she crested the top of the ridge, she heard the shrill beeping of a warning buzzer as a red light on her instrument panel started flashing on and off.

"Give me a break. . . ." She moaned. White clouds of smoke billowing from beneath the Jaguar's bonnet obstructed her vision. She slowed the car, instinctively gearing down into each transmission level until she pulled over on the wide shoulder. Smoke poured into the cockpit.

Tracey released her seat belt, unlocked the door, and leaped from her leather bucket seat. Fear charged through her veins as she assessed the situation. The smoke wasn't from a fire; it wasn't black or gray. She didn't smell the brackish odor of burning oil, so the oil line hadn't burst. There were no gasoline fumes, but an ominous hissing sound came from underneath, and the smoke looked more like steam.

Reaching inside the car, she grasped the handle on the driver's side to release the bonnet, then moved around the back, opened the passenger's door, released the second lever, and pulled it back. The bonnet popped open, allowing more steam to escape in every direction. The sickening-sweet odor of antifreeze and scalding water assaulted Tracey's sense of smell as it jetted from somewhere in the area of the radiator.

"Out here in the middle of nowhere. Great!"

She paced nervously around the car, then, as the steam began to ebb, lifted the bonnet fully open so she could peer inside. The entire engine compartment was soaked with radiator fluid and looked as if it had been blasted by a green-water wash.

Tracey shook her head and sadly viewed the interior. The highly polished manifold cover she had spent hours on last weekend glistened with a gooey green liquid. It dripped off the spark plug wires and covered the large battery. It was a mess. She peered down both directions of the vacant highway and contemplated her next move.

"I can't hitchhike and leave it here," she thought out loud. "No telling what would happen." Tracey kicked at the dirt, and tiny pebbles sprayed the gleaming chrome wire-spoke rims. "Too far from L.A. Mojave was the last 'big' city . . ."

A semi-truck and trailer sped by, blasting hot air and showering sand onto her and the Jaguar. She shook sand from her clothes, then checked the exposed side of the car for any sign of damage but, thankfully, found none.

"Can't stay out here, that's for sure."

Tracey shielded her eyes and surveyed her immediate surroundings. All she could do was sit and wait, and hope for someone with a cellular phone. Spying a large creosote bush that provided a smattering of shade, she headed toward it and inspected its base for snakes or lizards. She shook its wooden arms and, when nothing emerged, she sat down, folded her arms across her knees, and set up a vigil beside the broken car.

She watched helplessly as the vehicles that jetted past shook the Jaguar in their wake. A hollow feeling settled in the pit of her stomach. She realized how vast an area the desert was and how alone she felt, stranded there. She checked her expensive watch. Fifteen minutes had passed since she pulled over.

When the escaping steam slowed to a slight hissing sound, she returned to the car, dusting the back of her jeans. There was no more danger of being burned; all the fluid had dispersed. She prodded at hoses, jiggling them to check their connections, reached below the main hose, and drew back a greasy hand. Cautiously, she loosened the radiator cap and unscrewed it from its base. Inside the radiator, there was nothing but an empty black cavity.

She heard an engine gearing down, then the crunch of tires on sand, and glanced over her shoulder to see a series of red and blue flashing lights throwing erratic patterns on the side of her car.

"Thank goodness, it's the cavalry," Tracey said, relieved.

Absently drawing the back of her hand across her forehead, she realized she'd smeared dirt on her face. She quickly wiped her hands on the sides of her jeans and glanced at her reflection as it appeared in the mirrorlike glass. A maroon-colored ribbon held her ash-blond hair in a sideswept ponytail. Wrap-lensed sunglasses hid her gray eyes, but couldn't mask the heart-shaped face and cleft chin. In contrast to her polished look, a wide swath of black grease streaked across her forehead like war paint.

She took a second look at her rescuer. Tracey's throat constricted and her stomach puddled to her ankles as she focused on a flatbed truck that rattled and creaked as it arrived on the scene. A makeshift boom and hook wobbled as the driver slowed and stuck his arm out the window to signal his departure from the deserted highway.

"Oh, no."

Sunglasses, a thatch of thick red hair, and a beard hid the face of the man who approached her. Wearing faded jeans, he sported a plain blue chambray shirt rolled to the elbows, and long johns that were pushed up on muscular forearms. He had a confident air about him that Tracey identified in the bold stride.

Jann took one look and sized her up. *Mid to late twenties, no wedding ring or tan line on her finger—not married, or long ago divorced. Her perfume smells as expensive as her clothes appear. Probably makes good money, but at what? She has a nice figure—even those loose-fitting designer jeans can't hide that. Suede boots and sunglasses. She looks wary—but why not? She's a city girl, she's scared.*

He noticed Tracey's chin lift and her stance shift to that of someone used to taking charge.

He grinned. "Mighty nice car you have here."

The man looked at her with the appreciation of a sailor

on shore leave and acted as if he'd never seen a Jaguar, much less touched one before.

Uninvited, he craned his neck into the engine compartment. "Having a little trouble?"

"Uh, yes and no."

"Looks like you blew a hose."

"That's what I figured. How far is the nearest town?"

"About fourteen miles up the road. I'm headed that way if you'd like a tow."

"No," she blurted. "I'll get a truck out of L.A."

"Los Angeles?" The man scratched his head beneath the rim of his stained ball cap. "Lady, do you know how far that is?"

"I'm about three hours away."

"And about three hundred dollars," he calculated.

"Three hundred?"

Tracey's stomach knotted at the thought and she felt sick. Her head began to reel and her eyes smarted from the warm breeze that seemed like an unrelenting blast of heat from an opened oven door. She closed her eyes and struggled for balance.

"Are you all right?"

"I need some water." She reached into the baggage area of her Jaguar, pulled out a plastic container, and swigged on the wide-mouth jug.

"Unless you've got towing coverage on your insurance, and about four hours to wait, I can haul this into Inyokern for you and replace the hose."

Tracey momentarily juggled her fear for her personal safety if she chose to accompany this stranger with that of leaving her car as prey to thieves or vandals. She had towing insurance, but knew the company wouldn't pay the full amount. She didn't want the Jaguar damaged by this possibly well-meaning but inexperienced handyman. She was three hours from home—hot, tired, and on the verge of tears.

"I can't believe my luck," she murmured.

"What?"

Exasperated, she vented, "I don't know what to do. I've never been stranded like this before."

"You're on my way. Let me tow it for you. At least we can get your car off the road."

"But this is a *British* car. Do you know how to tow it?"

She imagined it being lifted up on that rusty-looking hook on the back of his truck and watching the beautiful front end being crushed.

"I'll take good care of it."

The man stood proud, confident, arms crossed over his chest and his feet planted firmly on the sandy soil.

"It's up to you. You want me to tow it or not?"

"You couldn't give me a ride, could you? I could call my shop from—what's the name of that town?"

"An' leave that car out here? Might not be a good idea. There's only one patrolman on this route, and he won't be back for a few hours."

"I don't have a choice, I guess. All right," Tracey conceded. "But *be careful* with it. My mechanics know this car as well as I do, and they'll testify for me if there's a scratch on it."

"Yes, ma'am. I'll have it out of here in a jiffy." He casually pulled on a pair of leather gloves. "Yessiree . . ."

Although she didn't feel free to voice her concerns, it bothered her immensely to trust her vehicle to just anyone. Since she had purchased the car, all the work done previously on her Jaguar had been performed by mechanics from the one shop she frequented in Santa Monica specifically recommended by the former owner.

The man's wide smile taunted her. She couldn't determine from the shaded eyes if he was to be trusted, but instinct dictated mistrust. She scrutinized his moves as he methodically unhooked the chain that held the sling in place.

Every fiber in her body strained with the alertness of a mother cat watching her kitten as the man operated the winch controls that lowered the hoist to the ground. He acted as if he knew what he was doing. Kneeling down, he peered beneath the car.

"There are two lower A-arms on either side of the front wheels," Tracey instructed. "You can attach your hook there."

He grinned and nodded.

When he tried to close the bonnet, Tracey injected, "Wait a minute, I'll go inside and latch it while you press down. We have to do it that way or it won't lock."

He bobbed his head. "Yes, ma'am. Whatever you say, ma'am."

"Don't push too hard. You might dent it."

It occurred to Tracey she might be interfering more than necessary, but her sole concern was for the safe delivery of her car into a decent shop until it was repaired and she could make it home.

The driver marched to his truck, wrenched the heavy door open, and slammed it shut behind him. He started his engine with a deafening roar and proceeded to back up, aligning the T-bar beneath the expensive foreign car. Tracey automatically motioned him backward, trying to guide the monstrous truck toward her prized possession.

"Not too close," she yelled above the noise.

The man stuck his head out of the window. "What'd you say?"

"Far enough," she said. Her stomach twisted as the huge rig moved backward, looming over her low-slung car. "No more, please."

"Four more feet?" He revved the engine menacingly.

"No more! No more!" she shouted, waving frantically.

He inched backward until she screamed, "Stop!"

The big truck lunged back and forth as its taillights glared into her eyes, indicating the brakes were set.

"Did I get close enough?"

"You almost hit my car!"

"Nah, I had plenty of room. See?" He waved his hand between her chrome bumper rail and his rear push plate. "A whole six inches."

Tracey was beside herself. This man had the sensitivity of a half-baked lizard. She almost expected to see him spit a wad of tobacco on her burgundy leather boots.

She stomped over to the creosote bush where she had taken refuge before and plopped down under its withering shade. She could see it did not help for her to try to assist him. It only made matters worse. She decided to leave it in his hands. If there were any complications, well, she'd have to deal with that when the time came. She propped her elbows on her knees and covered her face with her hands.

Chains rattled and clunked beneath her car. Every bump and scrape jarred her nerves, but Tracey bit back her words and cringed silently. In a short time, she heard the winch whirring as the cable pulled and strained to lift the heavy automobile from the ground.

The man operated the winch carefully, gently checking the tension of the chains before he raised the car higher into the air. He strung thick-cabled magnetic lights to the back fenders, then placed a single red shop towel on each side before setting the emergency lights on her car. It was all he could do to keep from laughing at his overanxious customer. Obviously, she was out of her element and scared. That his truck wasn't as fancy as any she might have seen in Los Angeles could be the reason she was upset, but he was pleased he had the opportunity to teach her a lesson.

Not bad looking, he decided. *Like most women concerned with their looks, she's not thin, but lean. She reminds me a little of Sheryl. Funny how it doesn't hurt anymore. There was a time I couldn't even say her name. After all this time I should have gotten over her. This one doesn't have that hard look around her eyes, though. Why hadn't I identified that predatory look in Sheryl?* He studied the woman whose worried gray eyes trained on him from her perch near the bush. She still wore the black streak across her forehead. *No.* He chuckled to himself. *She is definitely not like Sheryl.*

"Ready to go?" he called.

Tracey left her creosote perch. Her precious car looked like a wounded animal in traction behind the obscene monstrosity that had it bound and gagged. The truck's running board was high off the ground and difficult for Tracey to climb onto. She grabbed the door handle, pulled it open, then braced herself against the seat. At that moment a gloved hand pressed against her hip and pushed as she leaped into the cab, breaking the unwanted contact.

"Thanks," she said hotly, feeling color rise in her face. "But I could manage the step all right."

"Just tryin' to help."

Tracey wondered about that. A devilish grin spread over

his features, and although she couldn't make out the color of his eyes beneath the shades, she guessed that they, too, had a devilish glint to them.

"Here," he said, handing her a rag.

She looked at him quizzically.

"Your face."

She immediately peered into the large side mirror on her door.

"Oh my." Scrubbing her face with the rough shop towel, she chided, "Why didn't you say something?"

"I did."

Placing the dirtied towel between them on the seat, she glowered. "Thanks."

" 'Spect you'll be glad to be back on the road," he said as he started the engine.

The frown on Tracey's face didn't relax as she confirmed, "The sooner the better."

"Yep," the man drawled. "Most folks drive through here on their way to somewhere else. In a tremendous big hurry. Always comin' or goin'. Not much stoppin' 'less it's for gas or groceries."

She hadn't noticed it before, but her companion's hick-town twang irritated her. She crossed her arms and peered out the passenger window. For miles across the wasteland all she could see was the low, rolling hills of lava deposits and purple gullies dotted with sagebrush and scraggly looking desert plants.

"Got a name?" he asked.

"Tracey. You?"

"Jann."

"Jan? That's a girl's name."

"I've heard that before. Had to prove otherwise, too."

His amusement was infectious and Tracey relaxed a little.

"You say you're from Santa Monica?"

"That's right."

"L.A. gal. That's what I thought when I saw you. I could see it right off. Even without lookin' at that personalized plate."

"Oh, yeah?" Tracey's interest was perked. "How's that?"

Jann's gaze roamed over her from boots to head and back again before he replied. "Not many ladies 'round here dress the way you do. I mean, suede boots and all. Can't buy clothes like that in Johnson's dress shop."

Tracey looked down at her turned-cuff, low-heeled boots and the scoop-necked burgundy blouse she wore. Maybe she didn't look like she belonged in the desert. She was grateful for that.

"Your license plate . . . PURRRR," he repeated the word. "That's how your Jaguar sounds, right?"

The disarming grin and boyish charm of her companion broke the ice and she smiled at his blatant attempts at polite conversation. This guy might be a desert rat, but he appeared harmless enough. She caught herself checking his left hand for a wedding band, but his gloves hid that clue.

Tracey suspected that with his outgoing personality, he had married young. Probably had a passel of little desert brats playing in a weed-riddled backyard, she imagined, and a bone-weary wife who watched after them, toting a rake to ward off sidewinders.

"That is, when it's running, right?" he asked.

His question forced her to once again think about her predicament. "You guessed it." She sighed.

If he only knew how much money she'd put into that

car to keep it that way, he'd laugh at her all the way to the bank. Her friends in the Santa Monica Jaguar Club secretly called themselves the CCC Club—the Crying, Cursing, Complaining Club. It had become a personal joke reserved for the exclusive use of Jaguar owners who wouldn't admit outside their ranks how much time their cars spent inside the garages of Santa Monica's better repair facilities, and how little time was actually spent on the road.

"Yep. I knew a man who used to spend half his paycheck on his Jaguar till he totaled it coming off the Grapevine outside L.A. Said it was the worst day of his life."

"What happened?"

"A Volkswagen passed him going uphill." Jann chuckled. "It made him so mad, he floored it until he passed that Bug. Something blew, and the smoke got so thick he couldn't see anymore." Jann slapped his thigh, struggling to continue. "He drove it off the side of the road and into a ditch."

Tracey's driver seemed oblivious to her discomfort. She wasn't at all amused by the story.

"The guy must've been an idiot," she stated flatly.

"He was. He flagged down that Volkswagen and offered the owner five thousand dollars on the spot to swap titles. He's still driving that VW to this day."

"I don't believe that."

Jann held his hand to his heart. "I swear it's true. I know him well."

Tracey eyed the grinning man beside her. He was strange. Funny. But she sensed there was more to him beneath that lighthearted exterior.

As they made the turn east toward Inyokern, Tracey looked over the desert panorama with increasing awe. Spread out over miles of flat land, a city stretched in front of her, filling the entire vista. The immense size of the desert community surprised her.

"Is that where we're going?"

"Nah, that's Ridgecrest. The shop's in Inyokern, a little spot in the road down at the end of this hill. See it?" He pointed at a small gathering of buildings that seemed to grow out of a distant flashing intersection light.

"Oh, yeah."

"Why do you drive a fancy car like that, anyway?" His tone became serious.

"Because I like it."

"You can't fix it. A girl like you ought to have a car she can take care of in case of emergencies."

Tracey felt compelled to defend herself and her car against a man who obviously had no appreciation for the finer things in life.

"Haven't you ever wanted something so much, that you'd work and scrape and save until you finally got it?"

"Is that how it was with you?"

She squirmed in her seat, uncomfortable with the personal turn this conversation had taken.

"Yes. That's how it was until I finally got my Jaguar. No one and nothing is going to keep me from it."

"You know," he interrupted, then paused, as if weighing the wisdom of his next suggestion. "There's a man in town named Erikson . . . who could fix your car for you."

"Well, thanks, but . . . I think I'll call my Jaguar shop."

Jann eyed her reproachfully. "You'd spend that much money to have your car towed clear to L.A. when you're probably lookin' at a ten-dollar hose?"

Tracey fidgeted. He had a point. She didn't have money to waste on a tow if it wasn't necessary.

"You think so?" she asked tentatively. "You think he could replace it for me and get me back on the road?"

"I'm sure of it."

"Well, who is he, anyway? Has he got a business, or what?"

"Oh, he's a real foreign-car buff. He can fix anything with wheels."

"You mean from lawn mowers to Volkswagens?"

She watched Jann's jaw tighten while he digested her last remark.

"Nah. He's a real hotshot. Used to race cars. All over Europe."

"That's a laugh. . . . If he's such a famous race car driver, what's he doing out in the middle of this dust bowl, besides starving to death and living on dreams?"

"Maybe some people don't look at it that way," he replied slowly. "Most L.A. folks don't believe there's life outside the city limits. But it ain't the case."

"Well, if you're certain he's qualified to replace the hose, maybe I could make it home tonight."

"What were you doin' out here, anyway? You didn't come for the scenery, I'd guess."

"Not quite." She checked the view from her window again and then faced the driver. "Ever heard of Death Valley Dilemma?"

"You mean that road race through Death Valley?"

"That's the one."

"What about it?"

"I'm competing in it."

"You?" The truck swerved as Jann jerked his head sideways.

"Yes, me. That surprises you?"

"Driving that Jaguar?"

"I hope so. I was testing the area today to check it out—the road and all. I just hope I didn't damage the car. I shut it down as soon as the warning lights came on."

Jann's face took on a stern, thoughtful expression.

"I'm sure Erikson can fix it up for ya, ma'am. He's been around and knows lots about them foreign jobs. He's got the best 'quipment in town."

Tracey wasn't comforted by the man's boast. She wondered if Erikson's " 'quipment" was in the same shape as this decrepit-looking truck. She prayed the driver knew what he was talking about. Erikson seemed to be her only hope at the moment.

Chapter Two

The fourteen-mile drive into Inyokern was the longest ride of her life, of that Tracey was sure. Jann rattled on about everything from the weather, to the heavy Hemi-engine his friend was working on. She sensed he found her attractive, "for an L.A. gal and all."

"And what do you do?"

"Me? I . . . ah . . . just mess around the shop. Help out when I can. Pick up a car here and there."

"That's all you do? I mean for a living. What do you do to earn money?"

"Well," he drawled, "I don't s'pose you'd be much interested in that. After I drop you off, that'll be the last we'll see of each other. I'd bet you don't plan to stop in next time you're in the area just to say hello."

Tracey didn't know what to say. He was right. She would never deliberately go out of her way to stop in Inyokern. When she came through the desert again, she hoped it'd be on her way to the rally and back again. Hopefully she would be driving her Jaguar, not dragging it behind a tow truck. She quickly changed the subject.

"Is Erikson really all you say he is? I mean, does he work as a mechanic on cars like mine?"

"Only when they get towed in off the highway. Nobody in town owns wheels like yours."

"But you say he's familiar with exotic cars, like the Jaguar?"

"Yes, ma'am. Why, he raced for Porsche in the Monte Carlo Rally. You know, the big one?"

"Really?" Tracey considered this information. It was a stretch to believe that the ex-driver decided to shuck all the glamor and excitement that went along with being internationally famous. But still, if he were originally from the area and wanted to return to his roots, it was a remote possibility.

"I suppose if he's done all that, he must know what he's doing."

"Yes, ma'am. He just fixes cars for a hobby—doesn't need the money. Likes to take a piece of junk and work on it, just to see how nice he can make it. Why, I've seen him take the rattiest Austin Healy you ever saw, strip it down to the frame, sandblast the rust off, and start from the bottom up. Why, it was so purty . . . looked like it was drove off the showroom floor."

"And that's all he does now?"

"Aw, he makes so much money off his investments, I reckon he'll never have to work again. Not that racin' cars was ever work. For him it was like pushin' a baby carriage through the park."

As they approached the town Jann read aloud, "Welcome to Inyokern. Population one hundred fifty." He stuck his left arm out the window to signal his turn, even though they were the only vehicle on the road. They maneuvered the corner rather fast, with the Jaguar securely in tow, then stopped suddenly in front of an old metal building that looked as if it had been there since World War II.

"We're home!" the driver announced jubilantly. "Let me see if I can scare someone up."

A warm breeze lifted an errant piece of the rusty metal roof, slapping it back and forth, banging against its silent metal comrades. Fine, gritty sand swept around Tracey's face as she made the jump from the cab. Her feet hit solid dirt—hard, sunbaked earth. There was no landscaping at all, just a generous patch of tumbleweeds that looked as healthy as the Japanese cypress that decorated her meticulously landscaped condominium.

Tracey followed him around the side of the building. Over the doorjamb, she read a handpainted sign that heralded, JANN ERIKSON, PROPRIETOR. She gasped. *He couldn't be!*

Jann fit the key into the lock, but the door fell open beneath his hand.

"Hey, Torque, what're you doing here?"

Tracey joined Jann. She peered wide-eyed at the man behind the counter. Curled-toe cowboy boots with paper-thin soles were propped up on the desk. The owner was a wiry, suntanned old character who looked as if he were made up for a "Gunsmoke" set. He wore an ancient, stained cowboy hat severely rolled up on both sides. His denim vest barely met in the middle, looking as if it had shrunk several sizes. Above a salt-and-pepper grizzled beard, bright blue eyes twinkled with elfin merriment.

"Hi, Jann. I saw you light out of here like a whirlwind.

Thought I'd mind the phone. Didn't know you were bringing a lady friend.''

"You're Jann . . . Erikson?" Tracey confronted him.

"That's right, ma'am," Jann said, taking off his sunglasses. "Still gonna let me fix yore car?"

Tracey felt her face burn with embarrassment. "I, I—"

Jann chuckled, and a richness in his tone vibrated the air.

"Why didn't you tell me who you were?"

"I did."

"But you—"

"You wouldn't have believed me. Admit it."

"I don't know if I can believe you now."

He whipped his wallet from his back pocket and flashed an ID at her as deftly as any policeman flashing his badge. She studied the miniature face of a red-haired Erikson, Jann D., with an Inyokern address.

"You'll fix my car?"

"Trust me."

Jann's eyes were a splendid hazel color with amber flecks that danced when he spoke. The syrupy drawl he'd entertained her with on the ride over had vanished when they entered the garage. Tracey stared at him, confused.

"Somethin' goin' on here I don't know about?" Torque interrupted.

Erikson turned to his friend. "Torque, this is—"

"Tracey." She shook the older man's hand. "Tracey Evans."

"L.A. gal, huh?" Torque guessed correctly.

"That's right." Jann chuckled, and winked at the surprised young woman. "Come on, Torque. Give me a hand with this, will you? We've got a sick Jaguar to unload."

Tracey watched as the two gingerly unhitched the precious cargo.

"Get in and steer," Jann instructed. "We'll push it inside."

Tracey slid behind the wheel.

As they moved the car into position to enter the shop, Jann pulled the large garage door open with one swift movement. It was dark inside, but Tracey could distinguish what looked to be the back end of an expensive foreign car. Torque and Jann gave the Jaguar a final shove that pushed the heavy car forward into the small interior. Several banks of fluorescent lights flared at once as Jann tripped a lever by the door.

Tracey thought she recognized a vintage Ferrari. Glossy black, its smooth, rounded fenders disappeared into the sleek front end, not unlike her Jaguar.

"A Ferrari, or Cobra?" she asked.

"Ferrari. 1966 250GT."

"Yours?"

He nodded. His auburn lashes hooded the eyes that intently watched her.

"You're full of surprises, aren't you?"

"You're not," he said, his voice deadly calm.

"What do you mean?"

"I mean . . . Jann, the hick, couldn't come near your car, could he? But Jann, the racer—he's a different story, right?"

His face no longer held the humorous glint he'd shared on their ride over. It was masked in cynicism, maybe resentment. All Tracey knew was, the game he'd been playing was over.

Torque ambled in with his hands shoved in his pockets.

"Well, little L.A. gal, you ought to be thankin' yore

lucky stars you broke down where you did. Jann'll have you fixed up in no time.''

''Why don't you have a seat inside,'' Jann suggested to her. ''I'll check this over and let you know what I find.''

''If you don't mind, I'd rather watch.'' Tracey met his steely gaze with her own.

''Suit yourself.'' He reached inside the compartment and pulled the hood release lever back. ''Get the other side, will you?''

Tracey quickly moved around her car and did the same. She watched as he probed behind the radiator. Without saying a word he left the car, reached into a large tool chest, and retrieved a small screwdriver.

He loosened a small wire clamp and studied the freed hose. ''Think I found the problem.''

''What is it?''

''Bypass hose on the thermostat.''

Seconds later he unscrewed the other clamp, then pulled out a twisted piece of rubber hose.

''Is that it?'' Tracey asked, hovering over his shoulder.

''Yep. I think I've got a piece to replace this. That should put you back on the road.''

Tracey breathed a long sigh. She now knew how a young mother felt when her child just survived a first trip to the emergency room. ''Thank goodness that's all it was,'' she said, relieved.

''It's not over yet. We'll have to check it out and see if you've overheated the engine. You might have blown the head gasket. You lost every bit of your fluid. It was really hot.''

Tracey pulled the ribbon from her hair and shook her ash-blond mane. Her fingers ran through the hair from her temple to her crown, and she felt color draining from her face.

"It can't be blown. That'll put me out of the race."

Erikson cocked his head toward her and studied her anxious response. "I didn't say it was blown. I said I'd have to check it out."

She paced nervously back toward his office, winding and unwinding the ribbon around her index finger. "I think I'll get a soda. Do you have a machine?"

"Around the corner, to your left. Bathroom's on the right."

"Thanks," she murmured.

She took the right-hand turn into a bachelor's pad. The entire room was filled with a king-size water bed that faced a big-screen TV. A miniature kitchen with a bar and two stools comprised the eating area. The bathroom was a small shower stall, sink, and commode, all decorated in early flea market, according to Tracey's assessment. It looked as if Jann had removed himself from anything that reminded him of the fast-lane lifestyle he had led before. *But why?* she wondered.

When she emerged, Torque was on the phone, apparently talking with a crony, filling the person in on the Jaguar, describing car and driver in colorful detail. He winked at her as she walked past. Tracey felt she could be a friend to the old man. She'd bet he had a trunkful of tales to tell. Almost as many as Jann.

Jann, she thought. *Out here in the middle of nowhere. Doing what? Working on stranded motorists' cars? He must be crazy. Or very hurt. What kind of trauma had sent him from the arms of notoriety to Inyokern? What kind of woman would let him go? What kind of woman, indeed.*

Maybe he had followed a woman out here? Not likely.
Maybe he's running from one?

"All done." Jann's resonant voice boomed.

"Already?" she asked, startled.

"We'll fill her up, start her, and see how she runs," he answered nonchalantly.

"I gotta go," Tracey heard Torque tell his listener. "He's gonna fire it up."

She heard the phone drop, then Torque's boots clattered until he stood behind her.

"The man's got the magic touch with them automobiles. Ain't nobody can fix 'em like Jann." His wide grin exposed gapped teeth, yellowed with age. Myriad lines around his eyes told her he grinned a lot.

Jann had managed to imitate Torque's unique drawl perfectly, she thought, smiling. Tracey liked Torque, and was sorry she wouldn't have a chance to get to know him. It was obvious that Jann could do no wrong as far as Torque was concerned. Maybe she'd think so, too, by the time he was through with her car. She hoped so.

The two watched Jann fill the radiator with antifreeze, then twist and lock the cap. "Hit the key," he ordered.

Tracey smoothed her moist hands down the sides of her hips, before she opened the door and took her place behind the wheel. She turned the key and immediately the ignition caught and a loud *varooom* echoed in the garage.

"Whoo-weee," Torque hollered. He raked his hat from his head and slapped his knee with it. "You did it, Jann! What'd I tell ya, little lady . . . he fixed that ol' Jag slicker'n owl spit!"

Tracey's mood shifted from anxious to elated as she caught Jann's gaze. He seemed pleased with his efforts, modestly so.

"Let her run five minutes, then shut her down," he shouted above the noise.

He fastened an exhaust hose to the dual tailpipes and dragged it out the entrance. It muffled the steady idling sound slightly, but couldn't detract from the sheer beauty of the smooth-running engine. To Tracey it was the sweetest sound in the world. It really did purr. When Torque hastened to Jann's office, Tracey stepped from the cockpit over to the tool chest where Jann stood with his back to her, busily wiping his hands.

"Thank you, Jann," she said, moving closer. "I guess I owe you an apology."

"For what?"

"For not trusting you—for being scared."

"Don't worry about it."

"Tell me . . . why did you pretend to be someone else?"

"You really want to know?"

"Yes."

"To be blunt, you seemed so materialistic . . . classy car, fancy plates, expensive clothes. . . . Right down to your manicured nails."

Tracey felt her jaw drop. She shook her head, disbelieving.

"Tell me you don't paint your toenails, too? You do, don't you?"

"Whether I do or not is none of your business."

Jann continued, unaffected. "I guess I wanted to teach you a lesson."

"But you drive a vintage car . . . a lot more expensive than mine."

"Right. But when you met me you didn't know that. And I couldn't get to you at all, until you saw my car sitting here."

He stepped toward her and she backed up against his workbench, cornered. Tracey's heart raced and liquid heat coursed through her veins. Her gaze settled on the eyes that held hers and she saw an intensity there that replaced the casualness of before.

His voice lowered intimately. "Now I'd bet you wouldn't mind at all, if this 'hick' took you in his arms and—"

Tracey's hands came up against his chest and forced a space between them. "Back off, buster," she warned. "Nobody takes advantage of me. I don't care who you think you are."

She slipped out of his arms and stormed out of the garage into the bright sunlight. Tears pricked her lids and blurred her vision. She wiped at her eyes with her manicured fingers, eyed the glossy red polish, then balled her fingers self-consciously. Leaning against the powdery surface of the weathered building, she slid down its face and plopped unceremoniously onto the dirt where she sat and stared, unseeing.

The man was impossible. How could she deal with someone like that, pretending to be someone else, a wealthy man living like an ignorant nobody in a nowhere town? And then because she was obviously unattached, he thought he could take advantage of her, just because she was a woman. The more she thought about it, the angrier she became. *Who and what is Jann Erikson, anyway?*

The engine stopped, then Jann appeared at the front of the shop.

"We'll let it sit twenty minutes, then I can pressure test it—see if the gasket's blown."

He hunkered down beside her and asked, "Mind if I join you?"

"Are you sure you want to?"

Wordlessly, he assessed her.

"Go ahead," she conceded. "It's yours. I think."

"Listen . . . I'm sorry—"

"It's all right," she said, cutting off his attempted apology, then shifted her gaze to his.

"Let's start over, shall we?" He offered her his hand.

For the first time since she'd met him, she felt they were on the same level. His smile was as warm as the yellow-gold flecks in his eyes. The black cloud that hovered over her lifted as he offered her his hand.

"Friends?" he asked.

She placed her hand in his and felt the coolness of his large palm against hers, the earthy grain of the lines in his hand and the delicate touch in his fingers. "Friends." Her arm quivered and tingled when he slowly pulled his hand away.

"Hey, don't let me break up the party." Torque's toothy grin lit the face that peeked around the corner. His gaiety disarmed the emotions that surged between Tracey and Jann.

"Just introducing myself," Jann explained to his wizened friend.

"Well, move over, buddy." Torque proffered his hand also. "Welcome to Inyopatch, young lady." His dry cackle punctuated his greeting as he pumped her hand. Then he cocked his head toward the highway. "I guess I'd better head out. I hate to meet and run, but I'm goin' over to jaw with them pasta-slingin' gals."

"The Italian restaurant down the road," Jann translated.

"Nice place, maybe . . ."

"Nice to meetcha, little lady. Stop in and see us sometime, okay?"

Tracey hesitated then replied, ''I'll do it, Torque. Nice to meet you, too.''

She felt Erikson's gaze upon her as she watched his friend amble down the dusty roadside.

''Are you always so direct?'' she asked.

''I didn't mean to hurt your feelings.''

''I guess I asked for that,'' she admitted. ''I prefer honesty to whitewashing.''

''Then you'll forgive me?''

Tracey chuckled. ''You really have a way with women, don't you?''

A boyish smile feathered his lips.

''What are you looking at?'' she asked.

''If you don't mind hearing it . . . a beautiful woman.''

Tracey lowered her eyes and self-consciously rubbed her forehead. ''Is my face clean?''

''Perfect.''

''Torque seems like a lot of fun.'' It was her turn to try her hand at polite conversation. ''How long have you lived here?''

The ex-racer stared off across the street at a vacant lot that grew a tremendous crop of tumbleweeds.

''About two years—minus a couple of months. And you want to know why I'm living in a dust bowl like this, right?''

Tracey cringed. Her words sounded harsh when repeated. ''Are you . . .'' she ventured, ''living on dreams?''

''No. I came out here to get away from everything. And I found a place where no one would follow me. Does that seem so eccentric?''

From that perspective, Tracey understood. If he was running away from someone or something, they'd have to be pretty desperate to follow.

"Why here, though? Did you know someone? Had you been here before?"

"Actually, I found this place quite by accident. Almost the same way you did. I was on my way to Reno one night and lost an alternator up the road about twenty miles. I spent the night in the front seat of my car, and got towed in the next day. I called a friend from Los Angeles to bring an alternator to me. It would've taken two or three days, at least, to have one shipped in."

"You mean you got stranded here, too?" Tracey laughed. "That's funny."

"I didn't think so at the time. I had about the same opinion of the desert as you seem to have, but obviously, I've changed my mind. It grows on you. I can't imagine living anywhere else now. Especially not in the L.A. basin."

"Is this really all you do? You don't race anymore?"

Tracey felt her companion distance himself from her emotionally.

He stared across the street as if keenly interested in the nothingness that was going on. "I consult occasionally. Submit design modifications on spec to Porsche and Audi, but other than that, I've pretty much left the racing scene."

Silently, she assessed the man next to her. His burnished hair wasn't a true red, but an appealing blend of brown with auburn highlights. High, angular cheekbones and deep-set eyes gave him a noble Nordic look inherited from generations past.

A frown furrowed his Scandinavian features as Tracey observed him. It was obvious to her that some personal tragedy had propelled him into his self-imposed exile. It was then Tracey noticed something else. Unconsciously, Jann rubbed his gloved left hand with his bare right one.

As she began to ask him about it, he caught her gaze and quickly removed the gloved hand from his lap.

"You weren't, I mean . . . you aren't . . . married, are you?"

His mouth curled sarcastically. "Hardly." He was on his feet, acting as if he wanted to drop the subject. "I think that twenty minutes is about up. Do you want to stay out here, or would you like to join me?"

Tracey uncurled her legs and stretched to her full height, all five feet five inches, as she began futilely to wipe the dust from her jeans and follow Jann inside.

"What are you doing to it?"

"Got to put pressure in her, and if it leaks down, we've got a problem."

Jann screwed a strange-looking device into the overflow tank, pumped it up, checked his watch, then peered back at the engine, like an anxious surgeon observing his patient.

To Tracey, his garage looked antiseptic, almost as clean as an operating room. The walls were painted a high-gloss white; the bright fluorescents would have been envied in an operating theater. Different types of specialized meters and gadgets hung on stainless steel hooks that were strategically placed on the walls. The concrete floor shone; not a spot of grease marred the smooth finish. The inside looked more professional and better equipped than the Jaguar shop in Santa Monica. It seemed totally incongruous to her to have such a modern, up-to-date facility housed within the rundown shack it appeared to be on the outside.

"Why the disguise, Jann?" Tracey asked impulsively.

"I always dress like this," he defended himself. "It's not a disguise."

"Not only you, but the building. From the outside, you'd think this place was a warehouse for dusty furniture and rats' nests. But the inside . . . and you—no one would ever guess you'd been beyond this valley. What gives?''

"I already told you. I don't put much stock in keeping up appearances. And people who do"—he faced her directly and spoke in even, low tones—"aren't very high on my list of friends."

"You mean you don't associate with any of your old friends anymore?"

"Nope."

"Were they all that kind of people? Surely some of them were real."

"Lady, I can count my friends on one hand." He raised his bare right hand, emphasizing his point. "And most of them live right here in this little town." He returned his attention to the gauge. "There. It looks like your car's going to be okay. You're lucky you shut it down when you did."

"You mean it's going to be all right? No problems for the race?"

"Well, I'd suggest that you have your radiator checked. As old as this car is, you'd probably want to have it boiled and rodded out. And if I were competing, I'd have the tubes flared. Jaguars are notorious for overheating, and this desert will fry that engine."

Tracey pondered his advice. "How much would all that cost?" she asked, mentally assessing her savings.

"In L.A. I'd estimate over four hundred dollars."

Four hundred dollars. Tracey groaned. "I can't do that right now. The race is a month away, and I was saving for new tires."

"Well, if that radiator blows another hose, new tires aren't going to take you very far."

She grimaced at the thought of being stranded in the

desert again. Especially during the rally. Al Brack's face came to mind. How that man would gloat.

Just for a moment, she wished she had a sponsor like Brack had. He'd wrangled the Bakersfield Jaguar dealer, Marvin Jaguar, to back his vehicle in every Sports Car Club of America event for the past eight years. His car had free services and maintenance in exchange for the Marvin Jaguar logo that was airbrushed beneath the colorful SCCA sticker on the rear of his burgundy XKE.

"How much would it cost if *you* did it for me?"

"Me? What about your Santa Monica mechanics?"

"You're a mechanic, aren't you?"

"I'm a long way from L.A. You'd have to drive it up here and leave it for a while, till I could get to it."

"How soon could you do that?"

"Wait a minute. Don't you want to know how much I'd charge first?"

"Well, yes. You're right about the radiator. It's been running a little hot. I've been having trouble in traffic. It's stop-and-go most of the time, and—"

"Whoa." Jann chuckled. "Let's go to the office and figure this out."

She trailed him into the other room, and stood behind the counter while he checked the desk calendar for his appointments.

"I couldn't get to it before Saturday. As for the estimate, I'd probably have to charge you forty dollars for the parts and a hundred on the labor."

"That cheap? Are you sure?"

"Yeah. I don't have to make a lot of money here. That'll buy my groceries for a while." A boyish grin lit the flecks of gold in his eyes.

"You've got a deal."

"You mean you're going to drive three hours up here to let me fix your car?"

"Sure. It'll give me more time on the road, and you're going to fix it for half of what it would cost me otherwise. How much do I owe you?"

"Twenty bucks. That'll take care of the tow and hose. Now, when you do want to schedule the Jaguar?"

"How about this weekend? I can bring it up after work Friday. Could I get a rental car from—?"

"You won't need it."

"Well, I can't stay here. I'll have to get a motel."

"Whoa." Jann chuckled. "Your brain is on full alert, isn't it?"

"But—"

"I'll drive you to the motel. It's not that far."

"All right. It's settled. I'll meet you here about eight o'clock Friday night."

"I'll look forward to it."

His inflection sent goose bumps racing up her arms. As she turned, her long hair grazed her shoulders, and she thought she heard him whisper, "L.A. gal."

Tracey backed the car out of the garage and into the blazing sunlight. The engine sounded good from beneath the cocoa-colored bonnet as she revved it, and shifted out of reverse into first. She looked back and saw Jann leaning against the doorway of his garage, his arms and legs both crossed in an idle posture. She noticed he still wore the glove on his left hand. He returned her wave. Then she turned the corner toward the highway and eased out of his sight.

He stood and watched her until the Jaguar disappeared at the intersection. He hadn't met anyone like Tracey since—

"Darn woman," he hissed. Of all the places he'd been since the accident, he thought he'd be safe here. No one cared who he was or where he'd been. He could almost forget why he was here himself, until he ran into a woman like Tracey. Then he remembered, and it hurt. He tore the glove from his left hand and ran his fingers over the surface. Its scarred flesh had lost the pain long ago, but he hadn't. A woman like Tracey would have nothing to do with him. If she knew.

Chapter Three

"He actually *towed* your car? Then *fixed* it?"

"Ouch." Tracey flinched as her stylist yanked a strand of hair in her circular brush.

"Sorry." Lynn's apology was punctuated by a giggle. "You shook me up."

Tracey eyed her best friend in the large oval mirror in front of her. A tie-dyed silk sari swathed Lynn's shapely size-three figure in bright multicolored hues. Her hair was orange this week, and shaved around the ears and neck framing a delicate, flawlessly made-up pixie face.

"Guess what else?"

"Tell me, I can't stand it," Lynn urged.

"He's going to flare my tubes."

"He what?"

"The Jaguar's, Lynn. This weekend. He's going to flare the tubes in the radiator so the water can circulate faster. It won't overheat anymore."

"You amaze me. Who else but you could meet one of the most infamous males of the century and act as if he was nothing more than the guy down the street."

Jann's wide smile and reddish mop of hair appeared in Tracey's mind as if on command. It was his captivating amber-flecked eyes that held her thoughts, as Lynn held her breath.

"Is that all you're going to tell me?"

"How about we leave early for the race? We can swing by and you can meet him."

"Really? You think we could?"

"Why not? I promised an old buddy of his I'd drop by if I passed through there again. You'd have to see that place to believe it."

"You're on."

"Remember," Tracey said, "the race is three weeks away. I'm counting on you to navigate for me."

"Wouldn't miss it. Especially now that I'm going to meet Jann Erikson in the flesh!"

"You've got a clientele list that reads like a rock concert billboard, and you want to meet Jann?"

"He's *the* mystery man of the century," Lynn countered. "Rich, famous, party animal. Has an accident and drops out of society . . . There's a secret there. A deep, dark secret."

"I can't wait to see his face." Tracey laughed. "If he thought *I* looked like an L.A. girl, wait till he meets you!"

"Should I tone down my hair a bit?" Lynn eyed her colorful reflection in the large mirror and checked her hair, picking at the short strands.

"Of course not."

"How 'bout you?" Lynn grinned mischievously, holding up a handful of Tracey's ash-blond hair. "Shall we spike you up a bit?"

"No!"

"Come on, Trace. Just because you work at the most prestigious interior design firm in Malibu doesn't mean you can't change your look. You've kept the same color and style since you were in UCLA, and I was straight out of beauty school. Don't you want to change?"

"My employment status, Lynn. Not my looks."

"I was just teasing. You look great. I bet ol' Jann thought so, too."

Tracey smiled slightly. "Maybe."

"What do you mean, your employment status? Are you still thinking about striking out on your own?"

"All the time. It's not enough that I'm senior designer. I feel boxed in somehow. Like I'm not free to do *exactly* what I want."

"You'd be crazy to give up your job at M&M. They love you, Trace!"

"I know."

"And the money you'd be giving up!"

"Well, they have a sister store in Bakersfield—it's smaller, but they're having trouble finding a good manager. There's talk they'll sell it or close it." Tracey sighed. "I feel like I need a change. But I don't know. I guess it takes a lot more courage than I have."

"What? You're the most courageous woman I know. Single. Self-motivated, successful. Living in L.A. *That's* courageous if nothing else is. Driving a race car—"

Tracey remained silent.

Lynn snapped off the blow-dryer. "There you go. See you next week?"

"Right. My manicure."

"I can't wait to hear how the weekend goes. I want to hear *all* about it."

"It should be interesting." Tracey smiled.

Sliding behind the wheel of her car, Tracey thought again about Jann, standing alone as he watched her leave that night. She wondered what he had been thinking.

She barely remembered the long drive home that Sunday. It was as if the car had moved on clouds. She vaguely remembered turning onto Highway 14 through Saugus/Newhall before she caught the Hollywood freeway toward home. She had been surprised when she merged onto the Santa Monica freeway, thinking minutes had passed, not hours.

Automatically, she turned the key and started her engine. Could it be that she was falling for that desert recluse? How could she be interested in a man like Erikson? He had shunned all that was real and chose to live in a rundown shack and call it home. If the man was as rich as Lynn seemed to think he was, he had to be more than eccentric. He had to be sick.

Watch your step, the tattletale voice in her head cautioned. *He's not your type.*

But he was attractive, in a rough sort of way—his eyes, the innocent turn of his lips when he smiled, the wind-blown, russet-colored hair that waved around his collar. The shadow that clouded his past pulled the shade down on her thoughts and blocked her dreaminess.

He's a troubled man, the small voice insisted. *Stay away.*

Tracey found it hard to concentrate on her job most of that week. It seemed that if she didn't deliberately block it out, the image of the little shop in the desert kept edging its way into her thoughts. Before she was ready Friday rolled around, and she had an appointment to keep.

After fighting the Friday afternoon rush hour, she arrived home, unlocked her door, and burst into the refuge of her air-conditioned residence. It felt so good, after the heat and crush of the humid air and exhaust fumes from the highway, that she felt the urge to curl up on her queen-size bed and call it a night.

She tossed her keys into a shallow cream-and-crimson Indian basket that occupied the glass coffee table. She pulled off her snakeskin flats and felt the cool, smooth Spanish tile through her stockinged feet. A white ball of fur emerged from behind vertical blinds, purring loudly as it made a beeline for its mistress's legs. The silky, full-grown Angora cat rubbed itself against Tracey's ankles, curling its tail around her calf, maintaining contact as it turned and repeated the self-indulgent massage on the other side of its pampered body.

"Hi, Rasputin. Did you have a good day?"

The cat answered with a peevish-sounding, "Meow."

"That bad, huh? I'll fix a snack for you, then I've got to pack. You're going to be alone this weekend."

Tracey padded to her small kitchen with the cat in hot pursuit. Floor-to-ceiling windows bathed the vaulted living room in a pleasant, warm light from the sun's western exposure. Behind jade-colored blinds, a balcony overlooked Santa Monica harbor and the busy boulevard that paralleled the beach.

Tracey paid dearly for the privilege of that view but enjoyed every minute of it. Her job at Mason and Mignon's Interiors afforded her the means to access and purchase the latest Southwestern fixtures and accessories that graced her home. A circular, white sectional couch filled the spacious room, accented with turquoise, earth, and salmon-tone throw pillows. Handmade baskets from around the world were used for various purposes—one held magazines, one cradled an African plant, another held several alabaster eggs.

Tracey heaved a tired sigh as she wandered down the cool hallway to her large bedroom. That room also over-looked the ocean, and from where she lay at night, Tracey could view the stars when it wasn't foggy. The bed, in stark contrast to the white walls and living room, was meticulously made up in a bold, black bedspread with a luminous white lily abstract design that gamboled freely over the quilted fabric. The thick white carpet felt luxurious under her tired feet.

She removed the pewter-colored silk blouse she'd worn all day and eased out of a wool A-line skirt. Wearing only her camisole, half-slip, and hose, she lay back against the spread. *Only for a minute,* she thought. *I'll rest, then hit the road.* She closed heavy-lidded eyes, then exhaustion overtook her and she immediately began to dream.

Hot wind rushed by her face like a giant fan and blew her hair out the half-opened window. Tracey checked her speedometer as she moved into the winding curves. The powerful Jaguar's muffler roared, deep and throaty, like a wild animal's howl in the jungle night.

Tires screeched on the road as she took the curve hard and fast. She felt the car skid beneath the wheel when pea-size gravel covered part of her side of the road. "Easy, baby . . . easy," she coaxed. But the car continued to slide. "Oh, oh!" A bright ball of flame exploded in front of her, then—

Tracey woke, startled from her nap, with the sunset pouring through the sheers. A magnificent orange globe filled the sky where the sun began to disappear into the bay. She glanced at the slim, black designer clock on the nightstand that showed half past six.

"Oh, no . . . I've got to get going," she said aloud as she leaped from the bed. From her closet she pulled out a violet sweater and slipped into a pair of linen slacks. The flats she wore that day would have to do. She didn't have time to be particular. Grabbing her overnight case of cosmetics and a change of clothes, she ran through the living room and locked the door before it slammed shut behind her.

The traffic was more congested than it had been earlier that afternoon. Getting out of Los Angeles on a Friday night was a feat in itself. Being late only added to her distress. By the time she reached the Highway 14 turnoff, eight o'clock had come and gone. She estimated she'd be at least an hour and a half late. Maybe Jann would understand. She punched in his number on her cellular phone and listened closely as it rang several times.

The Jaguar ate up the miles as she cruised through the twilight toward her desert destination. The mighty engine hummed as she rode over the bypasses around several towns then shed civilization for the high desert. The car seemed to pick up momentum as the air changed from moist humidity to the dry, crisp air of the desert in spring.

The temperature outside rose with the change of environment. It seemed to Tracey that the Sierra Nevada mountain range formed a barrier to the clouds and moisture of the western side of California and kept it apart, not sharing its fogs with the vast open land. She rolled her window down and allowed wind to brush her hair recklessly back. It felt good to have the light-fingered massage pull at her scalp and skin.

Driving through Mojave, the hub city where one could

choose to go north, south, east, or west, Tracey calculated she was still an hour away. Her watch read quarter to nine. She didn't try to phone again, but gunned her car past the sign that proclaimed: *Bishop, Mammoth, Reno.*

When she arrived in Inyokern, Jann's shop was dark except for the mercury vapor light outside the door that bathed the entrance in a gloomy green pall. She left the engine running, got out, and checked the door. As she feared, it was locked.

I guess he thought I wasn't going to come, after all. I should have tried calling again.

At that moment, someone tapped her shoulder. She gasped and whirled around.

"Torque!"

"Howdy, ma'am," he said, dipping his hat.

"Oh, you scared me." Placing her hand on her galloping heart, Tracey leaned against her car.

"Jann said you'd be comin' in tonight."

"He's still expecting me?"

"I reckon. He said he was gonna clean up and change."

"Thank goodness. I thought he'd given up on me."

"Not likely."

"How long do you think he'll be? Should I wait for him here?"

"Can't say how long he might take."

"I made motel reservations. How far is Ridgecrest from here?"

"About seven miles," Torque informed her, pointing toward the distant lights.

"I could check in there and come back in the morning."

"Nah. Let's wait for him at the Sierra Lounge. It's a steak place down the street. Jann said something about grabbin' a bite to eat, too."

"That would be great. I am kind of hungry." She rubbed her stomach, which complained on cue about the lack of food. "I haven't eaten since lunchtime."

"Well, let's go then," Torque suggested. "I'll keep you company and beat off the rabble."

She climbed back into the bucket seat and leaned over the passenger's side to unlock the door for Torque.

"I ain't never rode in one of these Jaguars before."

"I promise not to go over sixty-five."

"Half a mile away? I hope to shout!"

She parked her car beneath the streetlight outside the tavern, then followed Torque inside the local hangout, a steak-and-ale lounge.

The Friday-night crowd filled the room with loud talk and laughter, mixing with the sounds of a piano player, waitresses shouting orders, and glasses clinking behind the bar. Several men perched on bar stools raised their hands at Torque, boisterously welcoming him while eyeing the blond beauty behind him.

"Who's the lady, Torque?"

Another whistled and howled.

"Jes' keep your hands to yourself," Torque barked. "Come on, darlin'. There's a table over here."

In the corner of the room, a table sat beneath a wooden wagon wheel of lights. Tracey chose a seat facing the door, while Torque placed himself opposite her.

"You think Jann will find us here?" she asked, her wide-eyed gaze roaming the crowded room.

"Sure as a rooster'll crow," Torque replied.

About that time a plump, pleasant-faced woman arrived with two menus and two glasses of water balanced in her hands.

"Howdy, Torque. You're on the wrong side of the room tonight, aren't you?" The waitress winked at Tracey.

"Nah." Torque grinned, flashing his uneven teeth. "Jes' keepin' the little lady company for a while. I'll have a cup o' coffee, Ramona."

"Make that two while I look over the menu." Tracey smiled.

When they were alone again, Torque removed his hat and set it on the place mat beside him.

"That's an interesting hat, Torque." Tracey smiled as she looked it over carefully. It looked as though it had served him longer than any hat had the right to exist.

"Ol' Buzzard Gut?" He picked it up and checked it from various angles. "This ol' Stetson and I been through a lot together. One of these days I'm gonna take it down to that hat cleaner on Ro-Day-O drive, fling it across his desk, and say, 'Clean and block that son of a gun; I'll be back in an hour.' "

Tracey burst out laughing. "You wouldn't!" she dared him.

"I'm tellin' you, before I die I'm gonna do it. But I don't think it's quite aged enough yet." Torque's cackle competed with the noise in the room.

The waitress returned with their mugs and perched her pencil on the order pad. Tracey ordered, then Torque started in again. "Well, I didn't think I'd be seein' you back so soon. You looked a might frazzled when you first arrived."

"You mean with my car riding on the back of Jann's truck?"

"I s'pose you weren't too happy at that."

"Like you said, I was lucky it happened when it did. Jann does seem to be an excellent mechanic."

Torque chuckled and his merry blue eyes danced. "Yep. We're right proud to have him in our town. Different fella, though. He don't let nobody get too close to 'im. Doesn't have a whole lot to say, but I'll tell you one thing for shore, ain't nobody will help you out faster'n Jann. He'd go out of his way to help a body out of a jam, and don't expect no pay in return, neither."

Tracey sensed the admiration that Erikson had fostered in this seasoned old man. He may have been a relic of bygone days, but Torque was a real man, one whose respect Tracey would like to earn.

"Has he ever told you why he quit racing?" The young woman edged closer to the table, noting the frown that crossed her escort's face.

"He had an accident. He kinda favors that one hand. But he's never talked about it. I only know what the townfolks said, you know, gossiped about 'im when he arrived. But that's all in the past. Nobody bothers Jann about where he came from or why. They's all jes' glad he came."

A loud chorus of laughter interrupted their conversation, and the subject was changed.

"Jann tells me you're gonna race that car of yours in Death Valley."

"Yes. I hope to place this year. I've made other rallies, but this is a big event for me." She thought about Al Brack, her biggest obstacle to a first-place win, and wondered if his car was outfitted and primed already. "I've always raced novice status before and unequipped, but this time, I bought a meter that ticks off the hundredths of miles so I can gauge my distance. My girlfriend, Lynn, is navigating for me."

"What do you want to race for? Seems to me you waste

a lot of scenery and gas goin' that fast to nowhere in particular.''

''I like it. It's exciting, and it's a challenge.''

''So is ridin' the rapids in a canoe without a paddle, but I ain't fool enough to try it.''

Tracey smiled. There weren't many people she knew with whom she could share her love of racing. It was usually a subject left unsaid, as it either inspired awe or disdain in the listener. She wondered if that was how it was with Jann. Although his racing profession was on a much larger scale than what she aspired to, did he find it garnered the same kind of response—glowing admiration and awe, or repulsion by the people he'd met? Who were the people he'd left behind? What was it he was really running from?

''Here you go, miss.'' The waitress returned with Tracey's order. While Tracey ate, Torque emptied another mug of coffee and kept a lively conversation going. A few minutes passed, when Torque shoved his chair back and grabbed his hat.

''Excuse me, ma'am, I think I drunk enough coffee today to sail the Queen Mary.'' Puffing his thin chest out, he swaggered a bit as he made his way through the maze of chairs and people toward the back of the restaurant. As she finished the last of her sandwich, another customer entered the building and gazed around the room until he found the eyes he searched for beneath a long blond wave of hair.

Across the room, their gazes met and Tracey felt an uncustomary shyness wash over her. Even better looking than she had remembered him, Jann wore a denim jacket and jeans. His auburn hair fell in casual waves that brushed his collar. His beard and mustache neatly trimmed, Jann looked pleased to see her, a small smile evident on his face until he approached her table. Looking at the half-full coffee mug across from her empty plate, it was evident to Tracey that he had hoped she was alone.

"Hi, Jann." Tracey greeted him warmly.

"Miss Evans." He said stiffly. "May I sit down?"

Tracey felt a little confused by his frosty manner. Did he not want to meet in a public place? Was he ~~was~~ upset she'd already eaten? *What?*

"You brought someone with you."

"No, I—" Before Tracey could explain, Torque came up behind his friend and slapped him on the back.

"Hi, ol' buddy. Glad you made it. I was beginnin' to bore this little lady." Torque's comical grin lit his face and his eyes twinkled mischievously. Tracey eyed Jann with amusement as she saw the scarlet flush that crept up the open neck of his shirt.

"That's not true, Torque. I was enjoying every minute."

"I was beginnin' to wonder if you'd make it, Jann. I was goin' back to the shop to borrow a crowbar to ward off these varmints. Tracey had every head in the place turnin' her way."

Jann grinned sheepishly.

"Thanks, Torque. I owe you one."

"Well, I'm gonna head out. Gotta catch up on my beauty sleep." He started to pull money out of his wallet, but Jann stayed his hand.

"I'll catch that."

"Mighty kind o' you, Jann." Torque shoved the old wallet into the back pocket of his well-worn jeans. "See ya tomorrow. You gonna be around, Tracey?"

"I don't know—"

"You'll see her again," Jann stated confidently. "She's got to have some work done on her car. And who knows how long that'll take."

"Yeah." Torque smirked, a conspiratorial gleam in his eyes. "That could take a mighty long time. Weeks... months."

"See you, Torque." Tracey smiled. "Thanks again."

"My pleasure, ma'am."

Hands in his pockets, the old man dodged friendly jabs with his elbows, matching jeers and jibes with the customers as he left. The waitress returned with water and a menu for Jann.

"Nothing for me, Ramona."

"Aren't you going to eat?" Tracey asked.

"No. I ate at home."

Tracey could see he had recently showered, too, by the wet curls at the edge of his collar. Without realizing it, her gaze followed the strong column that disappeared into the unbuttoned neckline. A portion of his chest was exposed and a damp smattering of curls lay close against his skin. The fresh scent of his shampooed hair teased her senses. Her eyes focused on the face that studied hers across the table. She wanted to explore the feelings he stirred in her, but reason overruled, and Tracey reined in her wayward thoughts.

"I'm glad you came," Jann said, low enough that only Tracey could hear.

"You didn't think I would?"

"I wasn't sure. But I took you at your word."

"Which was?"

"You told me you didn't say things you didn't mean. I waited all week to find out if it was true."

Tracey felt her stomach tighten strangely. "If I were a logical person, I wouldn't be here. I'm taking your word you can fix my car like you said you could. It might mean the difference in my competing in the race or not."

Driving three hours to have her car repaired by a man she really didn't know wasn't one of the smartest moves she'd made lately. Acting strictly on intuition rather than logic was something she was not altogether comfortable with. But Jann seemed trustworthy. She hoped he was as honest as she felt him to be. He might be as a mechanic, but what about man-to-woman? The effect he was having on her was not businesslike at all. Far from it. She felt compelled to keep their business relationship on track, even if it meant suppressing feelings that she wanted to nurture and express.

"Back to the race again, huh? Is that all you really care about?"

The smile he gave her was the one she imagined would grace the covers of magazines—the one that ensured a following of fans. It was a combination of youthful innocence and devastating masculinity. He reached across the table to slip his fingers under hers and rub his thumb over her knuckles. It was electric, and caused Tracey to tingle all the way to her toes. She felt a shot of fire surge through her, just from the penetrating look in his eyes and his unexpected touch. She withdrew her hand from his and took a long sip from her water glass.

"For now it is. I don't know you well enough for it to be anything else." She tried to ignore the solemn expression on his face as she reached into her leather clutch for her money.

"I'll take care of the bill," Jann said, picking up the receipt.

"That's not necessary," she said, retrieving it from his grasp. "I intend to pay for my expenses. You're saving me enough money that I can afford to do that."

"Suit yourself," he said, rising from the table.

She had probably hurt his feelings, she thought, judging from the coolness in his tone. But she wanted to make it clear from the start: business was business.

Tracey followed the Ferrari's taillights to his shop. By the time she arrived, he stood waiting for her, with the garage door opened and the lights on inside. She swung the long nose of the Jaguar into the bay, and savored the sound of the dual pack muffler as she revved the engine to ease it in. To her, it was the most beautiful sound in the world. The door closed behind her and she watched as Jann bent to lock it.

"Leave the key in the ignition," he ordered as he brushed past her into the office. "Fill out this work order."

She took the pen he offered and began to fill in the multiple blanks that asked for name, address, phone number, year and make of the car, etc., then signed the bottom line, and handed it to him.

He looked the invoice over, then tossed it carelessly on his desk.

"Did you make reservations in town?"

"Yes. The Starlight."

"Let's go."

The air was dry and balmy. A slight breeze lifted maverick strands of hair she had tucked behind her ear. He held the Ferrari door open for her and waited as she slid into the passenger's side of the plush bucket seat. Thickly padded, unlike the contoured leather buckets of the Jaguar, his seats seemed to envelop and caress her in an ultimate feeling of wealth and luxury. She took a deep breath and a long sigh escaped.

"Tired?"

"A little. It was a long week."

"Long ride, too, wasn't it?"

"I didn't mind."

After they'd buckled in, Jann adjusted the interior lights, looked over the gauges, and flipped levers, like a pilot preparing for takeoff, before he eased the big machine out of his drive. The Ferrari was so quiet, Tracey strained to hear the engine running. The interior was roomy and smelled of leather, new carpets, and Jann's cologne, making her feel sinfully pampered.

Diamond stars sparkled in the crisp, clean air, clearer than any she'd seen from her bedroom. Not a cloud interfered with the view given her through the curved windows of the elegant automobile. Tracey nestled into the seat, then surveyed Jann's profile silhouetted in the pale lights that emitted from the dash.

"This car is magnificent. What a beauty!"

"It gets the job done."

She imagined what Lynn would say when Tracey told her about this ride. She could see her friend's shocked expression and disc-sized blue eyes beneath that orange/red hair. Tracey giggled.

"What's funny?" Erikson eyed his passenger, then moved his gaze to the road again.

"I was just thinking about my friend, Lynn. She'd probably give a year's worth of free haircuts to get the chance to ride with you like this."

A smile feathered Jann's lips before he said, "Is she like you . . . a 'material girl'?"

"That's not fair, Jann. You don't know enough about me to say something like that. And I think you'd find you're wrong."

"I knew someone like that once." Jann's voice drifted in the darkness, and it seemed he spoke from a place in his memory that had long been put aside, but not erased from his heart. "I used to think she didn't care about things like that. But when it came to the test, she bailed out."

"What do you mean? What happened?"

"I was in an accident, Tracey. Maybe you heard about it? It's not important. What happened, though, was I learned about life and death and more important, what friends are made of."

"What does an accident have to do with your distorted opinions?" Tracey demanded.

Jann carefully maneuvered the powerful machine to the edge of the deserted road and yanked back on the hand brake, pulling the stick between the two seats. He impatiently switched on the interior light, filling the compartment with a blinding, harsh glare.

"What are you doing?" Tracey felt panic grip her heart, sending tremors of fear surging through her constricted veins. Backing up to the passenger's door as far as the unyielding seat belt would allow, Tracey braced herself.

"I used to think I was in love," Erikson snapped. "But after the accident, I realized I was being used. Imagine—a big, strong guy like me. I never thought it would happen. I was used to having women around. All the time. Uninvited. But I let one get close to me. She was good. It was marriage and kids and forever after—until the accident."

Tracey studied the face of the man, who looked tired and broken, wavering between tears and rage.

"She told me she couldn't live that way anymore—with the danger and all. But that wasn't it. She went straight out of my arms into those of the man who took first place that day. It wasn't me she wanted; she wanted a man who wasn't marked. A man who wasn't a loser. A man who didn't look like this!"

Jann thrust his left hand into the light, as if daring Tracey to turn her face. As beautiful as his right hand was, with long, square-tipped fingers and strength in the broad palm, his left bore a reddish mass of skin that looked as if a severe burn marred the flesh from fingers to the wrist. It wasn't a pretty sight. Her shock at the way he presented it to her caused Tracey to gasp in surprise. She felt his eyes upon her, watching her, as if testing her reaction.

Instinctively, she reached to smooth her fingers over the wounded area, but he jerked his hand away and back into the shadows.

"Don't," he ordered. "I don't need or want your sympathy. I just wanted you to know, that's why I'm wise to the pretenses people put on. Everything has to be just right with people like you and her. It has to *look* good, or it doesn't work. Right?"

He started the engine with an angry twist of his fist and peeled out of the dirt, sending a rooster tail of sand into the air. Jann kept his eyes fixed in front of him. The low car hugged the right side of the road as he sped into the darkness. Nothing more was said until he pulled in front of the motel and opened the trunk to retrieve her two bags.

"I'll pick you up in the morning," he said, after he deposited her luggage inside.

"What time?"

"Before noon," he stated, then roared away.

After she'd checked in and locked her motel room for the night, Tracey rummaged through her bag of clothes. Not finding what she wanted, she pulled out every piece of clothing she'd brought, but realized she'd left her nightgown. Exasperated, she threw the extra slacks and blouse on the bed, then carried her cosmetic case to the vanity.

Hairbrush in hand, she bent at the waist and began her nightly ritual of brushing her ash-blond hair into a thick frenzy. Her thoughts backtracked to the hostile confrontation in Jann's automobile. He really was sensitive about the disfigured hand, but it wasn't that bad, she mused. That other woman must have hurt him terribly. He had been deeply in love. But he had no right to compare Tracey with the woman in his past. She was different. And she would prove it to him. Somehow.

Chapter Four

Tracey woke to what sounded like gentle rapping on the motel door. The room was dark and her mind felt fuzzy and muddled. Forcing her eyelids open, she looked around the room then at her watch. Ten o'clock! She couldn't believe she had slept that late.

"Just a minute."

Sliding her bare legs onto the edge of the bed, she sat up and realized she couldn't answer the door. She was wearing only her blouse. The door rattled as if someone was trying the lock. She clutched the top sheet to her chest.

"Who is it?"

"Housecleaning," a male voice answered.

Tracey groaned and swayed unsteadily to her feet, pulling the sheet from its mooring between the mattresses. She shuffled across the carpet and opened the door as far as the chain would allow.

"I'm sorry. I'm not ready."

"Did I wake you up?"

"Yes . . . but I'll be right there."

"I'll wait for you in the lobby."

Tracey steadied herself against the door after she closed it. She couldn't remember when she had felt so fuzzy-headed after having a reasonable night's sleep. Probably just the change in climate, she rationalized. Or was it because she had slept like the living dead after calming herself enough to sleep at all? She had hoped to be ready before he'd arrived. But now, as last night, she felt at a disadvantage. It made her feel vulnerable and awkward.

She hurried through a shower, dressed, and made herself presentable. *How am I going to approach him?* she wondered. *Carefully. I don't want to risk another blowup.*

Never having dealt with a man like this, Tracey dug deep in her feminine center for the answers she would need to draw on. Jann wouldn't be easy to convince, but he might be a man who would prove to be a good friend in the long run. They had their love of automobiles in common, after all, and she had no other male friends outside the Jaguar Club who shared that interest. And if nothing else, he might teach her a few things about her car that would prove valuable to her in the future. And maybe the trade-off would be that she could convince him that all women weren't like his "Miss Winner-Take-All."

Jann tried to concentrate on the paper that isolated him from everyone who passed in and out of the lobby. *Got to hand it to you. Erikson. You sure know how to win the ladies over. After last night I'd be surprised if she even speaks to you.*

Jann checked his watch again out of reflex rather than curiosity. *If she's like any other woman, you'll be waiting here for an hour, pal.* His eyes felt gritty this morning from lack of sleep. He'd taken a long drive after he had dropped Tracey off, then when that failed to tire him, he spent the rest of his night working on her car and cursing the impetuous nature he'd perfected years ago—the same hard-driving, relentless devil in his personality that pushed him the final distance before the crash. . . .

She might consider giving me a second chance. She didn't look angry or vindictive. As a matter of fact—he chuckled—*she looked great. Sleepy-eyed and soft and cuddly, and*—

Tracey walked up and stood in front of the deep-seated vinyl lounge chair.

"Ready?"

Jann rose, setting the newspaper aside.

"Wow!"

He appraised the young woman from her snakeskin flats to the side part in her thick blond waves.

"That sheet didn't do you justice."

Her eyes narrowed and she ignored the comment, sweeping past him. "Ready?"

It was bright and beautiful outside. A few white clouds gathered on the Sierra Nevada mountain range west of the valley. The rest of the sky was a pale sapphire blue.

Tracey inhaled deeply. "What a great day. I'd love to be jogging along the beach right now."

"It's probably foggy down there." He opened the door to the black Ferrari and waited for her to get in. "The paper said a high of sixty-two—after the fog dissipates."

After he seated himself and started the car, she asked, "So . . . you keep track of L.A. weather, do you?"

"Only since last week."

She smiled at his admission, but wouldn't share the fact

she'd been listening to the high desert reports since then also.

"Breakfast?" he asked.

"I think I'll skip it. I need to wake up first. Can I help you with the car?"

"No need to."

"What do you mean?"

"Your car is ready."

"It is?"

"I couldn't sleep, so I worked on it instead. Finished about a half hour ago."

A sinking feeling settled in her stomach as Tracey understood Jann's words. She was disappointed. She wanted to watch him work on the Jaguar, since he didn't seem to mind. And without a reasonable excuse to shadow him, it would be impossible to implement her plan to get to know him.

"Would you consider touring the area, instead?" Before she could answer, Jann continued, "Don't say 'no' yet. It would do you good to check out the countryside, since you weren't able to finish your trip last week."

His face held that little-boy charm guaranteed to melt the coldest resolve.

"My services are available," he added.

Tracey raised an eyebrow. "Are you sure, Jann? You worked all night. Aren't you tired?"

"Not now. And I can't think of a better way to spend a Saturday. What do you say?"

"I'd love to." Tracey smiled.

"Great. We'll take 395 up to Whitney Portal. Did you bring a coat?"

"To the desert?"

"The temperature can drop to forty degrees this time of

year, and where we're going, that might be our high. I brought an extra for you, just in case.''

"We'll be gone all day?"

"It's an all-day trip up and back."

"Then I should plan to spend the night."

"I told them to save a room—you'd be back."

"Pretty sure of yourself, aren't you?"

Erikson just grinned.

Soon they were headed up the highway above the valley cruising on the ridge toward Mt. Whitney.

"How much of your Erikson story is true?" Tracey ventured to ask.

"All of it."

"You don't have to work anymore?"

"Only when I want to."

"You've left racing for good?"

"Totally."

"You never intend to go back?"

"Never."

"Talkative sort, aren't you?"

"When it suits me."

Jann's face creased into a reticent smile, and Tracey realized he was trying to be sociable. She could also tell he was maintaining a guarded distance.

She scoured the landscape trying to get a fix on her location. An uncomfortable silence ensued before Jann continued.

"Listen, I didn't handle myself very well last night. And it's bothered me."

Tracey's gaze met her companion's.

"I just wanted you to know I'm sorry."

"For what?"

"You're not making this easy, are you?" he growled. "My hand. I'm sorry I showed you the way I did."

"Is that why you couldn't sleep?"

"Partly. And with your car out of the way, I thought we could spend some time together."

"What if I'd said no?"

"I wouldn't have blamed you, but I'd have thought of something else. You don't mind spending the day with a bona fide former celebrity, do you?"

"You need a better line than that, Erikson."

Jann laughed and soon Tracey felt as relaxed as Jann appeared to be.

She appraised the man sitting beside her guiding the low-slung machine with light pressure from his fingers on the wheel. His burnished red hair flirted with the open neck of his knit collar, the same shirt he'd worn the night before. His jeans looked familiar, too; faded Levi's that buttoned down the front. He wore a gold-encased ruby signet ring on his right hand—the only jewelry in evidence.

His hands showed strength, yet had a delicate touch, almost like those belonging to a surgeon. It must have affected his ego to have one of his lovely hands scarred like it was. But he seemed unreasonably sensitive about it. Tracey knew that much, and it was a closed subject.

Jann cocked his head slightly and leveled his gaze on his companion. His left hand took the wheel, and he slid his right hand over hers where it rested on her thigh.

"Thanks for coming today."

He squeezed her fingers lightly, and she allowed them to intertwine with his. It was a comfortable manipulation, a pleasantness between friends.

"It feels good to be here. With you," she added.

Her eyes left his face and strayed to the desert plains outside the window.

"Doesn't look like much, does it?" he asked.

"Well—you just have to look a little harder, I guess. I'm sure it appeals to some people the way green trees and rivers do to others."

"I like it."

Tracey studied muted hues of ocher, violet, coral, and indigo that blended like watercolors on the hills before them. "It's like anything else—cars, clothes, furniture— some people like contemporary, some prefer Victorian interiors with tapestry and satins, Queen Anne furniture. Western is big now. Has been for quite a while. Indian patterns, soft desert colors, rough accents. Some of my clients like Early American. Unyielding, predictable curves and flounces. I use cotton fabrics for them—red, white, and blue."

"Yankee Doodle," Jann pronounced.

"Yes, indeed. There's a peacefulness to the desert you can almost duplicate in western furnishings. I kind of like the sparseness of it."

"It's a long way from L.A.," Jann stated.

"I grew up in old Santa Monica. It's a nice area, fairly quiet—I mean, it was. It's different now with all the people and their helter-skelter pace."

"I never thought I'd live up here," Jann admitted. "But now that I do, I'm not planning to relocate."

"Maybe that's why Hollywood stars moved to Las Vegas and Palm Springs—a refuge from reality. The quiet."

"All I need is my house and my car now."

"Do you think you'll ever get tired of it, Jann?"

"What? My car?"

"I was referring to the desert. Don't you feel a little too isolated?"

"No way. It's a long way from everywhere I don't want to be, and a short hop from anywhere I want to go. I still like to drive, you know. I just don't race anymore."

Tracey pictured him resting at home in the little apartment behind his shop. It just didn't seem consistent with how he had probably lived before, to give it all up and act like an impoverished nonentity in the back of a garage. She wondered about the man who caressed his smooth fingers over hers.

"What did you think about my car? Is it ready to race?"

"Well . . ." A sigh escaped his lips as he considered his response. "The radiator was worse than you realized. It was full of rust and corrosion. You were lucky you didn't blow the head gasket. But it's all right now. I flared the tubes. The radiator is good as new. The carbs could stand an adjustment. The battery looked okay. It should have new belts and hoses before the race. And those tires . . ."

She nodded. "I know. I already priced them. But like you said, I wouldn't get very far with a bad radiator. I had to make a priority decision."

"You don't intend to race with those tires?"

"I've already spent more on that car than I should have."

"When is the rally?"

"Two weeks away."

His expression grew thoughtful. "You ever been through the Alabama Hills?"

"You mean driven to Alabama?"

"No. The Alabama Hills. We'll drive right through them on our way to the Portal."

"You make driving seem so effortless, Jann. Like the car's an extension of you. Move and it moves with you."

"That's the way it should be. You're a part of that machine and you know every nut and bolt. You should be able to detect any change in the sound of the engine, or tires, and pinpoint the problem."

He guided her hand to the top of the shift knob.

"Here, feel this."

Tracey clutched the knob under her palm, but felt nothing other than the mighty hum. It sounded good to her.

"Feel that?"

She jumped slightly when the tires ran over a small rock in the road.

"That's incredible. I had no idea the shift knob was so sensitive."

"You can use it to detect all kinds of quirks. It just takes some practice and time to be able to differentiate between them."

His warm hand rested over hers, covering it completely. Slowly he lifted her curved fingers and pressed them to his lips. The tender gesture sent waves of pleasure streaming into her arms and upper body. Tracey studied the warm hazel eyes that swept over her face and hair.

"You know, you're very attractive."

She smiled a very self-satisfied grin.

"You shouldn't be out on your own like this. We might live in the twentieth century, but there are plenty of guys who act like cavemen."

"Like you, maybe?" she teased.

"Definitely."

Tracey wondered about the woman who'd left Jann. He seemed pretty sensitive about her after all this time, if it had been two years since his last serious relationship.

"Are you seeing anyone, Jann?"

"Just you."

"I mean on a regular basis. Is there someone else in your life?"

"Nope. You interested?"

"Just curious."

Tracy's mind wandered. She imagined driving with Jann on a long trip. Frolicking in a warm pool. Sharing a candlelight dinner. She shook the dreamy visions from her head. *We're a million miles apart emotionally, and might as well be that far physically.* He'd already vowed he'd never leave the desert. And Tracey knew that her work as an interior designer wouldn't have a place in this desert . . . or would it?

"You in a relationship?" he asked.

The question brought to mind her last date with Adam Eubanks, the spa owner she had been seeing. They had never quarreled, and he was pleasant enough to be with, but he could hardly qualify as the man in her life. Tracey's idea of a man wasn't "Mr. Huntington Beach," with biceps larger than her steering wheel.

"No. Just taking my time."

"Living at home?" Jann shifted slightly in his seat.

"No. I've got a good job and a place on the beach in Santa Monica. My friends and family all live there."

"So what prompted your interest in vintage racing? Or is this just a passing fling?"

"I've always loved old cars and I've always wanted to race. I don't intend to go any further with it than weekends with the SCCA, but I enjoy it. My mother is a great one for saying, 'Do it while you're young. We grow old too soon.' "

Jann laughed. "So, you grew up on Easy Street?"

"No . . ."

Tracey thought back to the beach bungalow where she and her family lived until she graduated from high school.

"No," she repeated. "Dad is retired now and Mom was and is a housewife. We didn't have it hard, but it wasn't really easy. Mom made all my dresses for special occasions, because the ones I wanted were always more than we could afford. She somehow managed to duplicate them, so it looked like we had spent a lot of money."

"Is that why you dress the way you do now? You never had it this nice when you were a kid?"

"I never thought about it like that. I've always liked nice things. I'm not trying to be anything other than what and who I am."

"Which is?"

"Tracey Evans, plain and simple."

Jann turned left at the Whitney Portal sign.

"Tracey Evans," he repeated. "Not plain. Not simple."

She ran her hands through the hair at her temples and shook the ash-blond cascade back, letting it fall against her shoulders.

"We're almost there. Are you hungry?"

"A little."

"I brought some lunch. We'll eat along the stream near the trailhead."

As they reached the edge of town heading toward the looming presence of Mt. Whitney, Tracey could see what looked like huge free-form statues jutting from the earth.

"The Alabama Hills." He smiled. "Hold on, I'll show you what road-racing is all about."

Jann downshifted and the engine responded with a throaty growl. Without slowing he maneuvered a curve, accelerating as he made the middle of the turn. Tracey could see the heightened state of awareness that overcame him as he switched into a racing mode. His face was a study in concentration, as he and the car became one. He operated hands and feet seemingly without thought as his actions became instinctive. It seemed to her they were driving on the two right wheels instead of four.

Tires squealed as they came out of the curve and started into another S configuration. She peered at his speedometer, which indicated sixty. The speed limit sign that whizzed by in a blur read fifteen miles per hour.

Jann gunned it as they drove out of the curve, then downshifted again into second, slightly tapping the brake before he entered yet another maze around the beautiful red rocks. As other cars approached from the opposite direction, Jann slowed his demonstration to a sedate speed, worthy of a retired gent on a Sunday drive. His whole body reverted to a calm, subdued energy level.

"That was fun. You make it seem so easy."

"It is easy." He pulled off the road at a turnout and pulled on the hand brake. "Here. You take the wheel."

"Drive your car?"

"Sure. Why not? I'll give you a few pointers."

"You'd never forgive me if I hurt it."

"You won't hurt it. Come on."

He clambered out of the driver's seat and around the front of the car to the passenger's door. Jann stood waiting for her to unbuckle her seat belt.

Tracey fumbled with the clasp. She reached behind the seat to unlock her door, then made another attempt at the belt that held her tight.

"Let me get that for you." Jann's arm brushed across her as he reached over and, with one flick, released the lever. That instant contact heated Tracey from the inside out as she tried to ignore the feeling that ignited from his touch. She accepted the hand he offered.

"Are you sure, Jann?"

"Don't be intimidated. My car shifts the same as the Jag, has brakes and a gas pedal. That's all you need to know." With light pressure on her elbow, he helped Tracey slide into the cockpit. He operated the seat lever and showed her how to push the seat forward to accommodate her shorter height.

After she was strapped in, he pointed out the different gauges and lights for her to be aware of, then he settled himself into the passenger's seat.

"I won't go very fast," Tracey told him.

"Get used to it first, then we'll see."

She felt more nervous than the first time she had gotten behind the wheel of the family car, with her dad as instructor. She looked around her and adjusted the rearview mirror, then eased the big machine onto the narrow strip of asphalt that was the road. The engine felt like a rocket beneath her hands, straining for blastoff. She applied light pressure to the accelerator, and it surged forward in response.

"O-o-o-o-oh." She gasped. "Sorry, Jann."

"That's okay. Get used to the horsepower. Just use a light touch on this. You almost have to treat it like you're flying a jet. You move, it moves."

Tracey took a deep breath and willed herself to relax. *Act like you're dealing with a tough sell,* she ordered herself. *Be nervous if you have to, but don't let it show.*

When she expelled her breath, her fears vanished and she propelled the car forward. There wasn't much of a margin between first and second, so she shifted right away. She rode about thirty feet with the clutch shoved in. The shift ratio was also shorter than the Jaguar's, and as she raised her foot from the clutch, the car lurched forward, eager to charge. Tracey felt red flags of embarrassment warm her cheeks, but she set her timidity aside, and took charge of the controls.

She pressed the gas pedal and entered a curve. It seemed they flew through the first one, and she accelerated harder.

"Tap the brake before you get into the next one."

Tracey touched the brake and the car slowed.

"No," he instructed. "Just tap it, until you find the solid bank of the curve, then gun it. You always want to ease into a curve to test it, then you accelerate hard."

Tracey shoved her foot forward, and the car zoomed through the tight S. She tapped the brake slightly before entering the next curve, then barreled out of it, eager to try another.

"You're a fast learner."

"I have a good teacher," Tracey responded.

It wasn't every woman who could handle a machine like that with the skill and focus that she exhibited. Jann was secretly pleased. There was something different about Tracey. She wasn't the cream puff he had originally believed her to be. Sheryl had preferred the passenger's seat to driving under any circumstances. She was a decoration, no more. Tracey, on the other hand, had potential. She had already proven to have more character and ambition than any woman he'd met. Even Torque approved of her.

"Do it again," he ordered.

Tracey narrowed her eyes on the fast-approaching curve, and downshifted from third to second. The compression roared from the muffler as they decelerated. Her foot weighted the pedal as she shot through the winding turn and into the open desert once again.

"I love it."

He smiled, looking pleased.

When she approached the stop sign, she looked for a turnout, but there were none in sight.

"Where do you want me to pull over?"

"Take it on up. It's not that far. It'll give you a little more time on this asphalt. Our roads have a little thinner base than those in L.A. Makes a slight difference in handling the car. You need to be careful not to oversteer."

Tracey waited at the intersection for a car to pass before she pulled out behind it, heading toward the mountains. She followed the speed limit, constantly checking dials in front of her, keeping tabs on the rearview mirror.

"Take him," Jann directed.

"Pass?"

"Any cars coming?"

She could see ahead for quite a while, and with no other cars in sight, Tracey stepped on the gas, and roared past the car in front of her. She could feel her cheeks strain against the smile that plastered her face.

"This feels so good. I love driving this car."

As they neared the base of the mountain, sagebrush gave way to piñon pine, then to shady scrub oak. Slowly, they drove up the road and into the park.

"There's a vacant spot." Jann pointed to the right. "Let's stop there."

Tracey pulled up into the parking lot, a fair distance from visible picnic tables and visitors. The brake was more sensitive than she was used to and they pitched forward slightly when she parked.

"Sorry. I'm not used to your brakes."

"That's okay." He grinned at his red-faced companion.

"You did real well for a beginner. You'll get better." He unfastened his shoulder harness. "Come on, I'm starved."

Tracey twisted her body out of the compartment. Clasping both hands together, she stretched them above her head. Lifting her face to the blue sky, she inhaled crisp, pine-scented air. As Jann had promised, a small stream gurgled beneath the trees on its way downhill. He rummaged in the back of the car, then extracted an insulated cooler and a thick blue Mexican blanket.

"Need some help?" Tracey asked.

"Nope. I got it."

Instead of choosing a picnic table, Jann bounded over a stream to a little grassy knoll. Tracey followed close behind, balancing on rocks in the creek then leaping to the edge of the grass. He shook the blanket free of its folds and spread it on the ground. On a beautiful background of royal blue, rows of woven red birds flew over the thick cotton fabric. Fringed in white, it had a simple, stylistic design.

As Jann unloaded the plastic-molded box, he recited jauntily, "A loaf of bread, a jug of wine, and thou, my sweet. . . ."

Tracey knelt beside him. "I never figured you for a romantic, Erikson."

She read the label. "Sparkling apple cider?"

He uncorked the bottle and poured the golden liquid into two tulip-shaped champagne glasses that he held in one hand, and offered her the long-stemmed goblet. "Skoal."

He tipped his glass toward hers, and Tracey repeated, "Skoal."

There was hope for him. She'd known it, intuitively. He could be tamed, drawn out of the shell he'd constructed around himself. He might even be worth the effort. At least everything they'd done together today told her so. Their eyes met over the rim of the glasses, and Tracey felt a twinge of longing. It would be easy to fall in love with Jann, yet so impossible. Their lives were as different as they could ever be.

"Like it here?" Jann asked.

"It's lovely. Hard to believe it's so close to the desert. What a contrast. It's cool, and moist. . . ."

She looked around at the tall trees that cast the park into cool shadows.

"Not at all as I expected."

"The desert's like that. It's as unpredictable and unbelievable as anything you can imagine."

"Kind of like you," Tracey decided. "I never know what to expect from you. Do you work at that?"

"Unbelievable?"

"Yes. And unpredictable."

He offered Tracey a wedge of cheese. "If you really wanted to, you'd get to know me in short order. But we're just two people who accidentally happened to meet, aren't we, Ace?"

He looked comfortable, dicing cheese in tiny triangles, as he leaned on one elbow. His legs were stretched out, crossed at the ankles.

"I suppose," she said between bites. "I never believe in chance, though. I believe in fate."

Jann sat upright then and stared into her eyes, intently studying the woman in front of him. "How are we going to manage being more than that when we live in two different worlds?"

"It could be a problem," Tracey surmised.

"It could be worked out," he suggested, leaning closer. "Ever thought of leaving L.A.?"

"All the time."

"So what's keeping you?"

"My family. My house. My work."

"You could visit your family. Better yet, let them come visit you."

"My house?"

"Houses are everywhere."

"Are you suggesting I move to the desert?"

"There are worse things. . . ."

"Okay. And my job?"

"I can't solve that one," he said, shaking his head.

Tracey felt the warmth of his breath on her, vying with the cool air that lifted delicate strands of hair across her face. She combed her fingers through her hair, tucking it behind her ear when Jann cupped the back of her head and lowered his mouth onto hers. Yielding to his kiss, she returned it with an equal sense of wonder and discovery. She could taste sweet cider on his lips and it made hers tingle all the more.

He pulled away with a strangled groan and nestled his face on her shoulder. "I can't believe I'm feeling this way. I never thought I would again."

Tracey caressed his bearded jawline, playing with the soft hair that curled against his cheek. He covered her hand with his and circled his other arm around her, drawing her closer. She felt the rapid drumming of his heart, and smelled the leather-and-spice cologne he wore. She raised her face to peer into the eyes that now looked almond-color flecked with gold.

Tracey felt swept away under the magic of the ancient pines. The capricious breeze that teased feathery boughs provided the music to their movement. It was an ethereal space, suspended in time, untouched by reality. She felt

Jann relax under her circling fingers. Tracey smoothed her hand over his arm, lightly gliding it back and forth.

"Kiss me, Jann."

"I want to," he whispered, nuzzling his face onto her neck. "But I'm not sure I'd want to stop."

She took charge of the situation and gently slid her hand to his face.

He turned his full attention on the woman's eyes and noticed how they had darkened to pools of liquid silver. It had been a long time. A long time of healing, of forgetting. Maybe someday, maybe with Tracey, he could even learn to forgive. He was scared. The thought of giving himself to a woman who might not be all he hoped took courage beyond all he'd known. He'd rather face a hundred contenders on an unknown course. At least he would have the familiarity of rubber and steel and asphalt to deal with. Emotions were something he didn't feel qualified to handle.

"We'll go slowly," she promised.

Jann felt his stomach tighten. He looked deep into her eyes and saw a diminutive reflection of himself. He experienced the mystical bond that united man and woman into an inseparable fusion of energy. They were more than when they started—they were becoming two halves of a whole.

Jann lifted his face from hers. He could see her eyes brightened by the intensity that drove them both. He smiled, seeing the watercolor wash in her glowing cheeks and the swollen appearance of her lips. Slowly, Tracey took a deep breath and leaned back, as if distancing herself. Idly, she outlined the bird pattern of the blanket with her fingertip.

"Time to go, huh?" He smiled as he struggled to gain composure, then drew himself up to a sitting position and reached for their forgotten lunch. "You get enough to eat?"

"Plenty."

"Me, too," he said, then busied himself rewrapping the block of cheese and refilling their glasses.

He raised his glass to hers and whispered, "Until later." The liquid trickled down his throat, as cool and satisfying as the kiss they had shared.

Tracey shivered. "Until later."

Chapter Five

Tracey covered a yawn with her hand, then shook her head. "I don't know what's the matter with me. I can't seem to get enough sleep lately."

"Worried about something?" Jann probed.

"No. I'm usually not like this. I get by on six to seven hours of sleep during the week. Must be this dry air."

"Well, we've got to move out if we're going to make Panamint Range and back before sunset."

"We're going there, too?"

"You wanted to check out the roads, didn't you?" His cocked eyebrow disappeared beneath a wave of auburn hair. "Of course, if you'd rather not—"

"Let's go."

Jann yanked the blanket by an end and shook it. Together they carried the picnic gear to the back of the car where he stowed it before taking his place behind the wheel. With the foothills and trees growing smaller behind them, the vast Owens Valley stretched endlessly, magnificent in lavender, taupe, and beige layers. The desert looked empty yet inviting as they sped past the Alabama Hills and into town. Instead of heading south, Jann steered the car toward the Panamint Range and Death Valley.

"It's perfect out here right now," he said. "January is Death Valley's tourist season, but in March, the wildflowers bloom. Have you ever seen the desert in full bloom?"

"No." She liked the smile on his face when he talked about the desert wildflowers, and mentally added that to the "Good" side of her Jann Erikson Good Points/Bad Points List. "They only bloom in March?"

"Yeah. They're gone by April, and by May, it's too hot to be out here tooling around."

"How hot does it get, really?"

"Try one hundred twenty to one hundred thirty-five degrees . . . in the shade."

"Not a whole lot of shade," Tracey added solemnly.

"February would be a good time for the rally. Twenty-four hours, didn't you say?"

"Yes. But that's over Friday night, Saturday, and Sunday. We'll have about forty-eight hours to do it."

"You'll need every bit of it, too," Jann said.

"We're not supposed to have any details ahead of time, and we'll get our instructions through the mail that week. All I know is, it's taking place in Death Valley. My girlfriend, Lynn, is navigating for me."

"She had any experience?"

"No. She's never been on a rally before."

The smile that edged his mouth told her he was amused.

"We're not a group of hard-core professionals," she explained. "Just ordinary people like myself who want some excitement and fun, that's all."

Jann picked up his sunglasses from the console and adjusted them on his face.

"Getting a little bright out here."

"It's so nice and warm, it feels good," Tracey said, shifting her body into the accommodating seat. She kicked off her flats and pulled one foot beneath her. "Mind if I get comfortable?"

"Whatever turns your wheels," Jann replied.

She closed her eyes and listened to the whisper of the car jetting through the desert air. Sometime later, Jann roused Tracey.

"Hey, sleepyhead. You're going to miss the sand dunes."

Tracey felt Jann's hand on her arm as he shook her awake. She rubbed her eyes, then looked out the window to see rolling hills of beach-white sand, as tall as one- and two-story buildings. "You're kidding me. I didn't know these were out here."

"Are you feeling all right?"

"I think so." She yawned. "Yes, of course I am. There's no reason for me not to be. I don't know what's come over me."

"Do you want to stop?"

"Do we have time?"

"We have all weekend." His devilish grin appeared again, as if he challenged her to take his dare.

"No we don't," she corrected. "I've got today with you, and it's been wonderful so far, but it's back to business for me tomorrow."

"Let's stop." Jann impetuously slowed the car and pulled over. When he stopped, he retrieved the blanket from the back and held his hand out to Tracey.

"What do we need the blanket for?" Tracey asked.

"I never go anywhere without it." Jann grinned. "Come on."

He took her by the hand and led her toward the first sandy mound that faced them. When Jann stopped to roll up his pants legs and remove his leather moccasins, she did the same, swinging her flats in her hand as they trod up the sunny embankment. The sand was as fine and clean as that along the beaches. Cleaner, she decided. It felt hot on her bare feet as they mounted the top of the hill. From there she could see miles of sand dunes that stretched into the horizon. The north side of the dune was washed in shadows that made it cool and deceptively moist. She plopped down in the shade, set her shoes beside her, and dug her toes into the fine earth, scooping it into her hands.

"This is great!" She laughed. "It feels like velvet, it's so soft."

Jann laid the blanket aside and joined her on the sand. Circling his arms around her shoulders and hair, he held her close.

"I thought you'd like this."

He held her so tightly, they formed a human cylinder.

"Hang on and keep your eyes and mouth closed." Before Tracey could protest, he swiveled his hips and rolled them down the shaded hill. Over and over, the world became a kaleidoscope of sky and sand until they finally reached the bottom and collapsed, laughing, in a tangle of arms and legs.

"Jann . . . you're . . . crazy."

"Bet you've never done that." He chuckled, brushing the sand from her cheek. He leaned back against the cool sand, clasping his hands behind his head.

"Oh, no you don't," Tracey scolded. "Let's do it again."

She reached for his wrist and willingly he allowed her to hoist him up.

"Race you!"

"After you slept in and had a nap . . ." He sprinted past her going uphill. "I'll still beat you to the top."

Tracey scaled the shifting sand, and made the top a few seconds behind Erikson. He reached for her again, but she slipped her hand into her pocket and drew out an elastic band.

"Let me tie my hair back first," she said, pulling her hair into a makeshift ponytail.

He drew her into his embrace. Her arms dropped comfortably onto his shoulders, then circled his neck as he lowered his face to meet hers.

Instinctively, her fingers began circling his shoulders, freely wandering the broad expanse of his back. His kiss deepened. Just as reality seemed to be slipping away, they knelt simultaneously and began the crazy descent downhill, like two children. Tracey felt as if she were wrapped in waves of clouds that held them like buoyant cushions and allowed them to tumble to the earth unharmed.

When they came to a halt, they hadn't quite reached the bottom of the hill, but were safely hidden in the shadows. The amber lights in Erikson's eyes flickered and burned mysteriously. His gaze held hers and spoke of a love that words could not achieve.

"Stay here. I'll be right back," Jann said as they disentangled arms and legs.

Tracey sat up and shook the sand from her ponytail, and began brushing it off her linen slacks.

"The clerk at Neiman Marcus would croak if she saw this."

She unrolled her cuffs and emptied sand that had become

trapped within the folds. By that time, Jann rolled back down the hill with the blanket wrapped around him. As he had at Whitney Portal, he flipped it out and guided it down in an airy spread over the sand. Eagerly, he took up a position on half of the blanket, not straying onto Tracey's side. He leaned back with his hands resting on his stomach, knees bent upward, and exhaled deeply.

"Ah . . . this is the life. Beautiful sky, beautiful sand, beautiful woman."

Tracey watched him settle into his spot.

"You're something else, Erikson."

Jann said, "I let you sleep, now it's my turn. Give me fifteen minutes, will you?" With that he closed his eyes, and drifted into sleep. His breathing slowed, then his face relaxed and his chest rose and fell, barely visible.

Dark-stemmed manzanita bushes grew in the gully at the base of the dune. Tiny green sprigs of leaves sprouted from what looked like dead wood, and a delicate breeze rattled the wooden branches of the plant, stirring tiny grains of sand in a circular motion. Except for the whistle in the branches, the desert was quiet in the extreme. Even Jann's shallow breathing was inaudible.

Tracey couldn't remember being anywhere in her life that was this peaceful. She didn't feel threatened by the silence, but it made her feel vulnerable to an element she didn't understand. She lay back against the coarse cotton blanket and listened to the silence. After a while, Jann stirred, and Tracey checked her watch. Twenty-five minutes had passed. It was time to go.

"Jann?" She touched his shoulder and he became alert immediately.

"Conked out on you, did I?" Erikson stretched his arms

and legs, reminding Tracey of her cat. He drew his wrist down to check the time, then sat up. "Let's hit it."

They trudged up the sand quietly, leaving the desert to its unending task of removing any sign that visitors had been there. After they reached his car, Tracey sank into the thick, cushioned seat and prepared herself for the final leg of their journey.

"We'll wind around Death Valley Buttes over to Hell's Gate, backtrack past Devil's Cornfield, then head down through Wildrose Canyon," Jann informed her.

"You sound like Lucifer's tour guide." Tracey snickered. "Maybe you could add that as a sideline to your occupation."

"If my clients were all as agreeable as you, that might not be a bad idea."

Jann winked at her as he started the engine and grabbed first gear, and they were off.

Tracey viewed the scenery from her window and saw what appeared to be bundles of straw growing from wedges of sand that had been sculpted by wind and time.

"What are those?" she asked, pointing to the odd-shaped vegetation.

"Devil's cornfield. It kind of resembles little bundles of cornstalks, doesn't it?"

Tracey felt Jann's gaze upon her, as she turned again to inspect the strange-looking flora.

"It's actually arrow weed. The Indians used those plants for their arrow shafts. See the stems?"

Tracey peered across the flats to the base of the plants and could make out what looked like rods about the diameter of her little finger jutting from the clump of long grass.

"I didn't know there were Native Americans out here."

"Used to be."

"How could they live? There's no water. What did they do for food?"

Jann's soft chuckle made his amusement transparent.

"There's lots of water in this valley if you know where to look. The Shoshone were the last Indians who lived in Death Valley, and they survived quite well. There are some rare bighorn sheep in the mountains, rabbits, ground squirrels, snakes. Things like that. I've seen springs in the gorges myself."

As they neared the southern entrance that opened up into the vast Panamint Range, the sun had already dropped to a low point on the western horizon. The sky became an artist's vision of muted pink, gold, crimson, and aqua streaks that spired from the incandescent orange globe that sat atop the Sierra Nevadas.

Tracey, although exhausted, dreaded the end of the day and their time together. Jann had allowed her to see him as a man—vulnerable, touchable, loving, and gentle. He had been all of that to her. She wondered what he thought of her now. Was she still the "superficial city girl" from L.A. whose motives extended no further than the repair of her automobile? Or was she more? Had she touched a place in his heart that had been scarred as surely as his hand had been? Would he deny that attraction now, as they neared their destination?

Jann seemed to sense her musings, as he interrupted her thoughts with a question of his own.

"Pretty full day, wasn't it?"

"I hate to see it end."

"Doesn't have to, you know."

Tracey placed her hand on his where it rested on the shift knob.

"Yes it does, Jann. You said it yourself, we're just two people who happened to meet."

"And fall in love?"

Tracey peered out the passenger's window at the last scarlet-orange fingers of light that burst from beyond the mountains. "It's not that easy, Jann. You've got your life to live. I've got mine."

"So. We're back to that again, are we?"

"Meaning?"

"Meaning, I'll never see you again, is that it?"

"I didn't say that."

"What did you say?"

"Jann, why argue the point? I'm living and working in L.A. What would you propose? That I quit my job? Move into the back of your shop? Hide in the desert with you?"

The air between them bristled. Jann seemed to be holding back an angry retort. She could've been kinder, she scolded herself. He had been nice in spades, and she repaid his generosity with harsh words. She felt angry with herself and remorse for him.

"Maybe I was." Jann's words spilled like oil on churning water, smoothing the waves. His boyish smile surfaced and he chuckled. "That would take care of the work issue. I could train you to be my assistant."

Tracey exhaled after holding her breath in anticipation of a hurt response from Jann. He didn't seem offended at all. Amused, if anything. The night sky was dark now, dotted with stars that shone like crystal chips against a curtain of indigo blue. Jann steered the Ferrari out of Trona toward Randsburg, but turned off on a deserted government road.

"I found this road one night." Amber dashlights illuminated his face. "It leads to a small radar station clear up on the top of the peak. You can see the whole valley from there.''

They wound higher up the steep, one-lane paved road that appeared well maintained.

''Is it public?'' she asked.

''The road is. The radar is fenced off, and there's a station of sorts up there, but I think it's checked only once a week or something.''

Jann must have sensed Tracey's hesitation, as he sought to reassure her. ''You trust me, don't you?''

''I don't know why,'' she admitted. ''But I do. If I were in the *city*, I'd know better than to put my life in a stranger's hands like this.''

Jann patted her hand. ''I know, but you're safe with me.''

Tracey couldn't explain why her actions were always at odds with reason when she was around Jann, but she did trust him. And she supposed she always would. They stopped at the top of the hill and parked beneath an enormous radar dish. The cool evening wind shook and rattled the fence that guarded the huge contraption, and whistled through the chain links.

Below them, the valley glittered with the twinkling lights of Ridgecrest in repose—not much traffic could be seen, but the streets were lit up like a miniature display. Above them, constellations seemed frozen in the heavens, carefully suspended in the infinity beyond.

''Orion is particularly clear,'' Tracey remarked. ''Look. There's Betelgeuse. See the star at his right shoulder? And Rigel, that's his left knee?''

''Where?'' Jann asked, craning his head to her viewpoint.

"On our right—his left knee," she said, pointing. "See it?"

"Yeah, I see it."

"And the Great Nebula surrounds the middle star in the sword. Can you see it, Jann?"

"How can you remember those stars?"

"How could I forget? Orion was the son of Poseidon. He was the handsomest of all men," she teased. "That was long before you, of course."

Jann leaned against the front fender of his car and opened his arms, allowing Tracey to snuggle back against him. The scent of sage carried on the breeze teased her nostrils. Silken strands caressed her face. Jann crossed his arms in front of her and pulled her closer. His heart throbbed against her back, sending streams of pleasure through her.

Tracey felt safe, wrapped in the security of Jann's arms. He warmed her, and if she could, this is how she'd spend eternity—lovingly in his arms. He shifted his weight beneath her, then Tracey stood.

"Too heavy for you?"

"No. Come on. Let's walk around a bit."

"I'm amazed the valley lights shine all the way up here. It's lighting our path."

"No pollution," Jann explained.

He scrambled over an outcropping of volcanic boulders that emerged below the station. Even in the darkness, Tracey identified graffiti that made it known this was a lovers' overlook. Hearts with arrows and initials, dates and forevers had been painted and scratched onto the molten surface.

She moved her fingers over a small etched piece that read, *T & D '73*.

"People are the same all over the world," Jann pronounced. "I stopped in a restaurant in France—a dive, really. At the front door the proprietor handed me a felt pen and pointed at the wall. One whole wall inside the restaurant was brick, and people had written messages from the floor to the ceiling. Just like this. No garbage, just love notes, signatures, and dates. It was great."

"Some people like letting the world know how they feel," Tracey murmured. "Others like to keep it inside."

Jann folded her in his arms and smoothed her hair down her shoulders, stroking her softly.

"Which kind are you, Tracey?" he whispered.

She raised her eyes, tilting her face upward, just as he bent to meet hers. His kiss was sweet and hesitant until he felt her respond to him, then he deepened it—slowly, torturously so. The breeze lifted her hair like angels' wings and swept coolness over them as they prolonged the kiss.

It was hopeless, he knew. But heaven help him, he loved her. Jann released a tortured sigh. "I better take you back to the motel. We've got work to do tomorrow. Might as well get some rest so we can get to it." His shoulders drew forward as he resigned himself to the situation. They were two people who just happened to meet and no matter how he tried to change that, she would still go back to L.A. and he would continue to live in the desert. Unless his luck was about to change.

Chapter Six

The mouth of the Jaguar gaped open as the rounded front end of the bonnet stood on its nose, exposing the interior of the engine compartment. The operation reminded Tracey of a checkup at a dentist's office, as Jann checked for loose bolts, looked for corrosion around the battery cables, and instead of using fluoride, applied a rust treatment to battery posts and terminals.

After Jann completed the minor tune-up, he carefully wiped engine grease from his hands and cleaned them at his sink. Tracey noticed he had not worn gloves since their trip to Mt. Whitney. He seemed relaxed around her, and much less sensitive about the scarred hand.

"Do you want the good news first or the bad news?" he asked.

"What is it? I thought it was running okay."

"It is, basically. As I said before, it needs a minor tune. The third S U carburetor needs adjusting, and I would suggest all the belts be changed before the race. That's the good news.''

"It is?"

"The bad news is . . .'' Jann paused.

"Give it to me straight, Jann.''

"I can't possibly get it done before two-thirty this afternoon.'' His fan-pleasing smile spread over his features, transforming his serious look into a sunny, captivating expression.

"Really, Jann? Is that all you were going to say?''

"Yes."

Tracey pummeled him while Jann shielded his torso with crossed arms.

"How could you tease me like that? You know how much this car means to me.''

Catching her wrists in midair, he drew her arms around his waist. Anchoring her to him, he kissed her playfully. She returned the kiss without hesitation just as she had last night. Tracey felt his warm chest against hers, her wrists held firm in his grip at his waist. She leaned into him, feeling so right within his arms.

Letting go of his grasp, Jann drew her closer. "I thought you were strictly business. A no-nonsense kind of girl.'' Jann's eyes glittered with the teasing sound of his voice.

"And you,'' she accused. "What happened to the man with ice in his veins?''

"I found a hot lady with a fancy set of wheels. What can I say?''

Their voices mingled in laughter as a third joined them from the front of the garage.

"What's all the caterwaulin' about?'' Torque loped through the open bay door wearing his Sunday clothes, a clean corduroy vest over a thin cotton cowboy shirt, his grizzled head adorned by "ol' Buzzard Gut." "Still introducin' yourself, Jann?"

Tracey tried to step back, but was held fast by Jann's possessive arms. She followed a crimson flush as it moved upward on Jann's neck through the open collar of his knit shirt.

"Nah, we got past the introductions all right. We're into the gettin'-to-know-you phase now."

Torque's high-pitched cackle filled the air as he slapped his knee with his hat.

Wriggling free, Tracey smoothed her clothing and strode toward the open door. "Maybe I better stay out of the way for a while," she suggested. "Let me know if I can help you, Jann. I'll be out here—"

"With me," Torque injected. "It ain't often I get to set with the likes of a purty L.A. gal." Torque winked at his friend. "We'll just set in the shade and pass the bull. Let you be about yore business."

Tracey's laughter rang in Jann's ears as the two left his shop arm in arm. Her presence filled him with an inexplicable warmth, and when she was gone—even just out of his sight—he felt an emptiness inside. Old familiar feelings of loneliness crept in without her to distract him. He shook his head and honed in on the job he had ahead of him. She had a race to run, whether he liked it or not.

After they settled in the shade outside, Tracey asked, "Tell me, Torque, what brought you out to this desert?" The muscles in her face ached from smiling so much. It had been a long time since she had felt this happy inside.

"Gold. That and silver. I started out in Darwin and then worked the mines in Randsburg. My Tilly and I raised our brood out there and I taught every one of my boys to be hard-rock miners."

"Gold? I had no idea."

"We never struck it rich. Never expected to. Tilly always told me she found her treasure in them hills when she met me. She died ten years ago."

A softer, faraway look filled his bright blue eyes. There was a serious side to Torque, after all.

"You don't have to talk about it if you don't want to," Tracey murmured.

"Ah, we had a good life, Tilly and me. My boys are all growed up and gone. Moved to the city and doin' fine."

"Do you think about joining them?"

Grizzled eyebrows shot upward and lost themselves beneath the stained rim of his hat. "No siree. I'm gonna live and die right here in this valley. No place on earth I'd rather be."

He patted Tracey's hand.

"Tilly and me . . . we loved the desert. I'd never leave either one of 'em." He heaved a sigh and drew the back of his hand across one teary eye. "That's enough about me. You and Jann seem to be plenty friendly. What do you think of that boy of ours?"

Torque's candid question demanded an honest response, but Tracey wasn't sure about her feelings. She had known Jann for too short a time for her to feel anything more than the obvious physical attraction they had for each other.

"He's a mighty fine fella, don't you think?" Torque persisted.

"He *is* nice," Tracey concurred.

"Not too hard on the eyes neither, is he?"

"Now, Torque," she scolded. "I don't need to have Jann's qualities pointed out to me. There's a lot more to a relationship than how a guy looks."

Torque's gap-toothed smile broke wide, and he cackled as before.

"That's what I tell the church widows. They just have to ignore that purty face o' mine and realize I got a heart o' gold in here, too."

Tracey shook her head.

"I'm not too long on manners, and I have to tell ya I like to shoot straight from the hip. I can see you're a real smart lady, and you're not about to be bowled over by just anybody."

She smiled.

"He's a good man. And from what I can see, yore a good little woman."

With that said, Torque began telling a string of tales that she suspected would keep her occupied for hours.

Jann heard Tracey's easy laughter several times as he worked on her car. Torque didn't take to many strangers, Jann was aware of that. It seemed curious to him that she and Torque hit it off so well. Their friendship solidified his gut feeling that there was more to Tracey than the sophisticated image she projected. She was a whole woman in every sense of the word.

He thought about the way she looked when she pried information from him about her car. The piercing, studied look in her eyes showed strength and focus. She had the concentration and intensity that befitted a racer and power in those slim, beautiful hands.

Jann thought about his own hands then, and subconsciously rubbed the left one. *What am I thinking about? Tracey wouldn't be here if it weren't for that stupid race. And when it's over, that'll be the last of us.* His self-conscious reproach dashed the loving thoughts he had entertained just moments before. Eyeing the vehicle as if it were a wounded warrior, he refocused on his task. It should be strong and powerful, as he saw it, not neglected, weakened, needing his care. He continued removing worn belts, laying them side by side, arranging them in the same order that he would install the replacements.

Angrily, he shoved thoughts of Tracey out of his consciousness and blocked the sound of her voice. Why? he wondered. It wasn't jealousy—not of Torque. But he refused to analyze it further. He'd get this car on the road and get Tracey out of his life once and for all.

It wasn't long before Jann finished his task. "You're all set." He stepped from the garage door into the shaded area where Torque and Tracey sat.

"You're finished?"

The gleam in his eyes was shrouded by a vacant look. Something had triggered Jann's emotional wall and locked it solidly in place. The casualness she had felt with him earlier had been put aside.

"What is it, Jann?"

"Your car is ready—tweaked, tuned, and primed."

"Well," Torque drawled, "that didn't take long." He pulled at his shirtsleeve and checked his watch. "Whew. I'm as windy as a sandstorm in July. I've got to get crackin'. I promised the good sisters I'd help out at their potluck this afternoon."

"Thanks for keeping me company, Torque." Tracey pecked his cheek.

"Jes' remember what I said, little lady. Don't forget about us after you leave this valley."

"No chance of that."

"See ya later, Jann," Torque said, then ambled away.

Jann had already retreated when Tracey turned around then followed him inside. His shoulders bowed with the suggestion of self-protection and it seemed to Tracey he was deliberately avoiding a face-to-face encounter.

"What is it, Jann?" she repeated.

Keeping his back to her, he seemed preoccupied with the tools he wiped. "What is what?"

"What happened in here? Did you want me to help? Maybe I shouldn't have been sitting around when I could've been helping you."

Jann whirled about impatiently, but instead of responding, his gaze settled on her. He seemed tired, resigned.

"The car is fine, Ace. There's no problem. Here." He handed her a fistful of wrenches. "Help me put these away, will you?"

Tracey marveled at how quickly the amber flints sparked in his eyes. How could he act so angry, then switch to his tender, gentler side so quickly? His mood swings puzzled her, but he seemed to be back on track. She watched as he methodically replaced the screwdrivers, sockets, and crescent wrenches, knowing which drawer to open as he'd probably done a thousand times.

"I guess you'd better head out," Jann suggested.

"What about my bill?"

"We can take care of it later. I can mail it to you."

"That wasn't the deal. I came prepared to pay."

"Have it your way."

She waited until he emerged from his office with a bill for her car.

Tracey felt a tugging at her heart. It was time to say good-bye, and it was proving to be difficult.

"Jann, I had a lovely time." She reached her hand out to him as if to offer a handshake.

He looked at her proffered hand then back into her eyes. "Back to business now, eh?" Taking her hand, he pulled her to him, pressing her face against the solidness of his chest.

Tracey felt his heart beating steady and sure. She inhaled the pleasant leathery cologne he wore. The masculine scent suited his strong and sensitive personality and she knew she would always associate it with Jann. He fingered a strand of her hair and her scalp tingled. She didn't want to leave, but mustered reserves of willpower to send her forth.

"Be careful, will you?" His voice wavered as if on the verge of breaking.

"I'll see you again soon, Jann."

"When?"

"The race is two weeks away. Lynn and I will stop by if we leave early enough. She wants to meet you."

He stiffened and pulled away.

"She want my autograph, too?"

Tracey knew he had turned on a defense mechanism to distance himself from the emotions he was feeling. But his words sounded vicious and scathing. She searched his eyes for the truth behind his speech, but found the blank expression he used when he was hiding from hurt.

"I better get going." She sighed. "The traffic—"

"Yeah, I know."

Jann shoved his hands into his pockets and leaned against the workbench. Tracey felt his eyes upon her as she placed her bags in the back of the car, adjusted the mirror, and strapped herself in. Their eyes met briefly, and she gave him her bravest smile.

"Thanks again, Jann."

He nodded.

She turned the key in the ignition. The loud *varoom,* as it caught, sent a chill through Tracey's body and she shivered. She had been warm outside. Almost too warm, but now she felt cold. She put it in reverse and backed it out into the brightness of day. She let the engine warm up, and listened to the rhythmic chatter of the well-tuned machine. It sounded good.

Jann had taken a position against the doorjamb, arms folded loosely across his chest. He smiled, but it seemed his heart wasn't in it. Tracey fixed her sunglasses on her nose, tied her hair back, then took a last look and waved. The Jaguar seemed eager to be back on the street, and it reacted instantly as she pressed her foot on the gas pedal. Jann disappeared from view as she came to a stop, then turned right toward the mountains.

As she entered the highway, Tracey's frown deepened on her forehead. Something was troubling Jann, but what? Surely he didn't believe they could be anything more than a chance meeting in the middle of nowhere. She had tried to tell herself that also, but her heart wasn't listening. *He probably thinks I was leading him on,* she guessed. *But I wasn't. We're both adults, and if we're stupid enough to fall in love with the wrong person, then we'll pay for it.*

And pay for it she would, Tracey knew. She cupped her hand over her mouth and coughed. Her throat felt dry and raw, and it seemed her temperature was rising. She reached for the small water jug she carried in her car, unscrewed the cap, and drank deeply.

The big engine purred loudly, just as it was designed to do, and Tracey thanked Jann again silently. She was lucky to have found him, but he would have to take his place in her memories now, if her mind would cooperate. She doubted it would.

Jann kicked at the dust outside his door. She'd done it again. His gut felt as if someone had slammed a steel fist into it and left him concaved. She took his heart with her when she drove away this time. She wouldn't be back. He'd seen to that. He practically insulted her at the last. She wasn't a woman who deserved to be treated that way.

"Idiot!" he cursed himself.

Jann marched into the garage and pulled the Ferrari door open. Jamming the key in the ignition, he fired it up and backed out. He lit the tires in front of the shop and roared off heading north, the opposite direction from Tracey's destination. He had to get away.

Tracey's digital alarm blared, rousing her from a deep, dreamless slumber. Her fevered hand ached as she reached to switch off the noisy clock. Awake, she turned on her side and felt as if her entire body was a collection of aches and pains. Every joint throbbed with unfamiliar hurt. Throwing covers aside, she attempted to sit up, but the room swam in front of her. Gently, she lowered herself back to the pillow, damp with perspiration.

"Oh no." She moaned. "I can't be sick. I've got an appointment today."

Rasputin meowed and stretched next to her bed then rubbed his fur on the side of her mattress.

"Go away, cat. Let me die in peace."

The cat continued its insistent meowing.

"All right, I'm coming. . . ."

Pressing fingers to her throbbing temples, she made her way to the back door and let the cat out. She should be at work in half an hour. Tracey's head reeled as she sat down heavily at her small table. Her fingers trembled when she dialed Mason and Mignon's office. The answering machine intercepted her call and Tracey tried to speak, but her voice was faint. She left her message, asking that her appointment be rescheduled, then managed to get back to bed. The rest of the morning passed without her knowledge until she finally woke again after noon to a growling stomach. Hunger forced her out of bed and into the kitchen in time to answer the telephone.

"Hello," she rasped.

"Tracey, it's Donna. We got your message and Mrs. Carr has rescheduled with you. Is Wednesday all right?"

"I hope so. I feel awful, but surely this'll pass."

"Got the flu?" Donna asked.

"I think so. I slept in over the weekend. I didn't realize it at the time, but I was probably running a fever."

"Well, you just rest and drink lots of fluids. It's been going around."

"Thanks, Donna. I'll check in tomorrow."

Tracey mixed a cup of broth and drank it, before returning to her bedroom. She drew floor-length sheers aside and gazed across the beach at the Pacific. Graceful waves rolled in, scattering seagulls from their sandy perches. As always, the street below bustled with a stream of bumper-to-bumper vehicles and people—walking, jogging, riding bicycles— all "hurrying to go somewhere else," as Jann had put it. Her gaze shifted to the jade-green ocean, lapping at the shoreline. She opened the sliding glass door a few inches hoping to hear waves crashing on the shore.

She lay back against the welcoming comfort of her bed and tried to block the sounds of the street and listen only to the ocean's muffled thunder. Her thoughts returned to Jann. She hoped he hadn't caught whatever bug she had carried. What would he be doing this afternoon, and what about tonight? She drew the pillow over her face and tried to sleep, but his laughing voice and playful eyes wandered among her thoughts like clouds scuttling over the bay.

* * *

Jann dialed the Santa Monica number for the second time in two days.

"Mason and Mignon's," the receptionist answered.

"Miss Evans, please."

"I'm sorry, she's not in. May I take a message?"

Jann's frustration and curiosity drove him to probe further. "It's urgent that I reach her. Hasn't she been in at all?"

"I'm sorry, sir, but Ms. Evans is ill. We expect her in tomorrow. May I take your number and have her return your call?"

"That won't be necessary." Jann hung the phone on the cradle and furrowed his brow. Tracey was sick. But he wondered with what, and how serious it might be. He picked up the handset and dialed.

"Torque, this is Jann. I'm going to L.A. tomorrow morning. Will you keep an eye on things for me?"

Torque seemed pleased to be able to help and said he would.

"Good. I'll be back Thursday."

Jann mentally made plans to facilitate his impulsive decision. He would see Tracey tomorrow if it meant tracking her to her home.

On Wednesday morning, Tracey felt as if she had been given a second chance at life. The virus that ravaged her for the past two days had passed, and she felt almost as healthy as she had before it consumed her. Rasputin even seemed to be in a more pleasant mood, meowing softly as Tracey shooed him off her bed and onto the floor. She clasped her hands in front of her and then stretched high above her head, standing on her toes. It felt good.

"Wow," she exclaimed, viewing the rose-colored sky.

Long vermilion slashes of clouds streaked the opalescent sunrise, and foamy white froth edged the waves like rows of French lace on a lady's petticoat. She pulled open the sliding glass door to let Rasputin out for his morning escapade.

"Hurry back, cat. I've got to leave today and act like I work for a living."

The regal Angora ignored her as it darted between the cream-colored sheers to the balmy air outside.

After a long, soapy shower, Tracey pulled on a pale satin robe and peered at her reflection in the bathroom mirror. A natural pink hue again rouged her cheeks and a sparkle lit her round gray eyes. She splashed cold water onto her face and gasped as the icy droplets clung to her porcelain complexion. With eyes closed, she groped for the fluffy hand towel on the rack and patted her face dry. She quickly curled her hair and spent twenty minutes under her portable bonnet-style dryer. After it had dried, her hair required a few vigorous brush strokes that left it gleaming in loose waves around her shoulders.

She chose a blue silk tailored blouse and a nubby linen slacks-and-jacket ensemble. A single strand of pearls and earrings accented her outfit. Tracey downed a quick cup of coffee and cream cheese on a bagel, and called it breakfast. Just in time, Rasputin returned so Tracey could lock up and leave without having to hurry on her first day back to work.

At the glass fortress of Mason and Mignon's, Tracey pulled samples of carpet, linoleum, and tile she had promised to show Mrs. Carr, then raced to the rambling Malibu beach house. The showing lasted nearly two hours as they pored over variations of tone and texture to complement the casual but expensive California interior. Mrs. Carr's tastes aligned with Tracey's and they settled amicably on pieces that Tracey had brought.

Driving back to her office, Tracey whizzed past popular seaside restaurants that tourists and stars frequented. Had she been entertaining a client, Tracey might have stopped there herself, but today she would settle for something easier on her stomach, like instant soup. She wheeled the company van into the back parking lot. With her arms full of samples, she struggled to open the metal door, then propped it open with her knee.

"Maybe that's her now," Tracey heard Donna say.

Tracey peered over the top of her load and straight into a pair of autumn-colored eyes.

"Jann!"

His eyes lit up when he saw her, and he strode around the counter to remove some of the burden from her arms. "Here. Let me help you with that."

Donna eyed her with mock suspicion. "Are you going to tell me you were home sick all this time, Tracey?" Donna's face looked like a cartoon character's from beneath her blue-tinted eyelids and mop of blond corkscrew curls.

Tracey felt her face flush with embarrassment, but ignored Donna's insinuation.

"How are you doing?" To her, Jann's resonant voice sounded like rolling waves cresting on the shore—soothing, strong, and steady. "Are you all right?"

"What are you doing here?" she asked, startled.

"I heard you were sick. I was in your neighborhood, so I thought I'd drop by."

"My neighborhood?"

"I was hungry for seafood," he said, flashing his heart-stopping smile. "You haven't eaten yet, have you?"

"If she has . . . *I'm* free," Donna interrupted.

"I'll be back in an hour," Tracey said quickly, amused by Donna's reaction.

The young receptionist propped her chin in her hands and sighed at Tracey's date as they walked toward the front doors.

"Please hold—"

"My calls," Donna finished. "Yeah, I know."

Jann grinned as he held the door open for Tracey and gently guided her out.

"Shall we take my car?" Tracey asked.

"Well, I thought we'd take both. I have something in mind, but I'd like to discuss it over lunch."

"Sounds serious. Is this business or pleasure?"

"A little of both," Jann admitted. "But first let's eat. I can't concentrate on an empty stomach."

They drove in separate cars to a cramped, cozy seaside restaurant that utilized the same chrome and red Formica-topped booths that had been there over forty years. An assortment of glassware and black-and-white publicity stills of Hollywood stars decorated the wall above a twenty-foot counter. The place was almost filled to capacity even though it wasn't quite noon.

"You were sick?" Jann asked, looking concerned.

"I'm okay. Touch of the flu." Then feeling guilty, she asked, "You didn't come down with it, did you?"

"Nah. I'm okay. Just hungry."

"They serve the best deep-fried shrimp on this strip," Tracey whispered over the top of her frayed menu.

"Sounds good," Jann murmured. "Is that what you usually have?"

"When I want shellfish. But clam chowder sounds good to me today."

After they had placed their order, Tracey could contain her curiosity no longer.

"What are you doing in Santa Monica? Are you here on business?"

"Well, you might say that. You see, I ordered Pirelli tires for the Ferrari a couple of weeks ago and I have a proposition."

Tracey's eyes rounded in curiosity. "What did you have in mind?"

"I was wondering if you'd do me a favor."

"What kind of favor, Jann?"

"Well, you know I don't drive as often as I'd like. I didn't want to take the Ferrari on a long trip without breaking in the tires. Your tires and rims are the same as mine. I know it's asking a lot, but would you be willing to run the Pirellis on the Jaguar for a couple of weeks? When you're through I could mount them on my rims, and not have that break-in period when I take that trip to San Francisco I'm planning."

Unaware she had been holding her breath, Tracey released a long sigh of relief when Jann had finished his proposal. His initial hesitation had mistakenly led her to believe he had something a little more romantic in mind. She then considered his offer and it roused suspicion.

"What you're really saying is, you don't want me to race with those half-bald Michelins I'm using. Is that it?"

"Well . . . I really had ordered the tires. I was going to replace the ones I've got. It wouldn't hurt if you used them during the race then dropped them off afterward. Would it?"

His bashful grin disarmed her. Secretly she felt elated that he had gone to all this trouble for her.

"That's generous of you, Jann, but I can't accept. You really don't need those tires right now, do you?"

He reached across the table and stroked her balled fist with his long fingers. "I need the tires," he stated, his deep voice modulated above a whisper. "And I'd like you to use them."

"But you've done so much for me already."

"The tires are a loan. I'm not out anything and neither are you."

Tracey eyed him cautiously, not knowing how far she should accept his charity. "No strings?"

"No strings. No lines. No ties that bind and gag. Just an offer."

"One I'd be stupid to refuse."

"Does that mean you will?"

"How can I lose?" Tracey asked. "I want to win that race so bad, I'd almost hock the Jag. Almost."

"Well, that wasn't as hard as I thought it would be." Jann chuckled. "You've got yourself a deal, Ace."

The waitress delivered their lunches and the conversation ended. After the plates had been removed, Tracey regarded her companion with narrowed eyes and asked, "Why are you doing this? I thought you were dead set against my racing, and now you seem to be supporting it."

"Let's just say, I'd like to give you a chance, that's all. I hope after you've given it your best shot, you'll give it up and go back to whatever it is you like to do. Like shop for new clothes and decorate your fancy condo. A condo on the beach, right?"

Tracey felt her face fall at the impact of his words.

"Is that all you think this is to me? A fling? I almost believed you had faith in me as a driver. A competitor." She slammed her soiled napkin onto the table. "You're as bad as Brack and his cronies. 'Move out of the way, give the little girl a chance,' " she parodied. "Well, let me tell you something, Erikson. I'll make that race without your charity and without your snide remarks. I'm going to prove I'm just as good a driver as they are. Even if I don't have the background and the financing like they do. It takes more than money to get the job done.''

"Hey," Jann soothed. "I didn't mean it the way it sounded. Don't get so worked up.''

Her eyes speared him over her raised water glass.

"C'mon. I know that race means a lot to you. It used to mean a lot to me, too.''

He looked out onto the ocean, and a faraway expression settled on his face. He rested his chin on his scarred hand, then self-consciously removed it from her view and covered it with his good one.

"My last race . . .'' His voice faltered, then he cleared his throat and continued. "My friend, Armand, and I were running first and second. We drove into a thunderstorm near Bremen, Holland that followed us into France. Outside Nice, there are some hairpin curves that are hard to control at a decent speed. We were pushing it. He was right on my tail.''

Jann choked up, vaguely aware of Tracey, but he wasn't in the Santa Monica restaurant. He was in France, reliving the incident as though viewing it on a video.

"My Porsche started to fishtail . . . it was raining so hard the wipers couldn't keep up. A cliff dropped to the sea on my right, a mountain on the left. Armand tried to pass. I blew a tire and lost control. I don't know how I stayed on the road. I was spinning end for end. I don't know how many times. His car hit mine then he spun out. He hit the wall and—''

Jann's eyes held the vision of his friend burning in the wreckage and his heart weighed like a pound of cement. His throat tightened into a ball of pain as he relived the incident. He closed his eyes and swallowed, but the ache grew larger. His eyes burned again as they had in the crash, hot salty tears behind closed lids.

"I tried to get him out—" He covered his face with his hands then allowed his fingers to smooth his wrinkled brow and rest over his eyes as if trying to hold back the flow of tears. "I tried. . . ."

Tracey placed her hand on his arm.

"The car exploded when I reached for him. That's the last I remember," he whispered. He inhaled deeply and with the sigh came an audible, primitive sound from deep within. His face grew stony and as he regained control, his eyes grew sharp and hard. "But I've got this," he growled, rubbing his thumb over the mottled flesh, as if trying to stretch it smooth again, "to remind me every day . . . I lost my friend. My career. Nearly lost my life."

Moments passed before he rejoined Tracey in the present. Heaving a sigh, he cleared his throat. Gradually he became aware of the clanging plates and lighthearted chatter around him. With his control locked into place, his voice gained clarity and volume.

"I don't want you to race, Tracey. Don't you see, it's your pride or ego you're feeding. You don't have to race to prove something to yourself or anyone else. You can be who you want to be without the trophies, fans, notoriety. What are you trying to gain anyway?"

Tracey wasn't sure how to respond. Jann's confession was tragic and she sympathized with his agony over his friend's death, but that was an experience in his past. She had a future to look forward to, and her dreams included participating in the race.

"I'm doing it for fun," Tracey started. "I want to have a good time. But I also want to prove something to myself.

I want to feel what it's like to do something I've always wanted to do. And win. I want to win."

Jann's eyes blazed. "You haven't heard anything I've said, have you?" His voice rose as he continued. "I figured as much. I didn't think I could talk you out of it." He released an angry-sounding sigh. "That's why I'm here. I'll put tires on the Jaguar and you'll make your race. I hope this dream of yours doesn't mar that beautiful face to the point you can't look at yourself in the mirror every morning. Or worse, put you in your grave."

Jann shoved his chair backward as he stood. "One of these days you're going to realize that Tracey Evans is underneath all the masks you wear. Nothing matters but what's inside, lady. And that's what I'm hoping to find."

He wrenched the ticket from the table and marched to the register to pay. Tracey stared at the cold coffee in her half-filled mug, and wondered what she should do next. Before she mustered herself from the table, Jann returned, pocketing his change. He flung his keys on the table.

"I need your keys."

Tracey fished in her leather clutch for the single set of tiny British keys and held them up.

"I'll get the tires mounted and deliver your car when they're finished." He turned his back on Tracey and walked out to her car.

Tracey shook her head. *What did I do this time?* She understood now why Jann quit racing, but why was he so violently opposed to her amateur racing? She was gaining nothing but the satisfaction of attaining a goal, or at least trying. What difference should that make to him? Or to anyone for that matter?

She couldn't afford to refuse his loan of the tires. She would figure out a way to pay him back, but for now, she had no choice but to accept his offer.

Chapter Seven

Before Tracey was fully inside the large glass doors, Donna converged upon her.

"Who was that man? And what are you doing with his Ferrari?"

Donna's large blue eyes widened with exaggerated curiosity. Tracey would've laughed at her friend's comical expression, except her heart felt like lead in her chest.

"A friend," she answered dully. "We've traded cars for a couple of hours."

"Traded?" Donna's disbelief showed. "I know your car is nice, Tracey . . . but a Ferrari for a Jaguar?"

"Any messages?" Tracey asked.

"Just one." Donna's voice returned to its normal monotone pitch. "Brenda Marlow called. She's a friend of Mrs. Carr's and wants to schedule a consultation. This afternoon, if you can."

Tracey's mind shifted to business as she tried to concentrate. "I'll be in my office, Donna. Thanks."

She swept past the receptionist's desk and picked up the message slip from her mailbox as she went. Closing the door to her glass-partitioned office, Tracey separated herself from the showroom. The pearls around her neck felt icy compared to the burning warmth she knew colored her skin. Her forehead beaded with perspiration and she pressed shaking fingers to her brow and decided she probably wasn't completely free of the virus. Or was it Jann's tirade that raised her blood pressure? Regardless, Tracey was determined to behave as if nothing had transpired to upset her usual calm demeanor.

Her fingers flew over the push-button digits as she dialed Brenda Marlow's number. The turmoil of the last hour dissipated as Tracey put her professionalism to work. Minutes later, she rushed out to the showroom and snatched the samples she had shown Mrs. Carr.

"Got to run, Donna. Brenda Marlow's house. I'll have the van back by three . . . I hope."

"The van's gone, Tracey. Merle has it in Pacific Palisades this afternoon."

Tracey stopped halfway through the back door as she realized her plight. She did an abrupt about-face and strode through the plush, carpeted interior.

"Let Jann know I had to take his car to a client's home. Keep him occupied till I get back, will you?"

"With pleasure!"

"I'll hurry," Tracey said.

"Take your time," Donna answered as the doors swung closed.

* * *

It was late afternoon when Tracey returned and nosed the glossy Ferrari to the storefront. Her car was parked on the side with four brand-new tires mounted on the polished chrome wire spoke rims. The car shone. Jann had obviously found Classic Car Wash, which excelled in handwashing and waxing luxury automobiles.

She opened the Ferrari's passenger door and retrieved the bulky samples. Donna and Jann were nowhere in sight as Tracey pushed open the thick glass doors with her elbow and her foot. She dumped her parcels onto the floor and strode through the showroom to the elegant lounge.

Donna rearranged magazines while Jann appeared completely absorbed in the *Architectural Digest* he was reading. A crystal goblet rested on the African teak table at his side. It was evident Donna had served Jann the expensive Chablis that was reserved for VIPs.

"I'm sorry I'm late," she said. "It was an unexpected appointment I couldn't afford to miss."

Jann set his magazine aside and stood up. The anger he had exhibited earlier was now gone, replaced by a calmer, apologetic manner. She didn't know how to read him. Tracey had felt this energy of his before, and well knew the happiness or its unhappy equal when it surfaced. Now, she only felt the magnetism that seemed to increase in intensity as he neared her.

Donna excused herself and left the two alone in the lounge.

"I haven't been here long." Jann took three long-legged steps that placed him directly in front of her. He held out his hand. "Friends?" A lock of reddish hair curled over one eyebrow and his expression asked for forgiveness.

"Friends." Tracey accepted his hand and her smile

broke the tension she had been feeling. His touch was soft and cool next to her warm, moist one.

Pulling her into his arms, he held her briefly then led her back to the plump green velvet couch where they sat and held hands.

"You washed and waxed my car," she stated, glancing out the window at the Jaguar.

"It looks like 'it drove off the showroom floor,' " he teased, mimicking Torque's drawl.

Tracey giggled self-consciously as she remembered their first time together in Jann's truck.

As if he read her mind, Jann's eyes sparkled and he urged, "Come on. Let's get out of here."

"Where?"

"Your place?"

"I don't know." Tracey hesitated. She searched his face for any indication she shouldn't invite him, wavering between reason and caution. "I'm not in the habit of inviting men to my home, Jann."

"I understand," he murmured. "No problem."

Tracey fought with herself as Jann tipped the crystal to his lips and drank the remainder of the wine. He had never forced himself upon her, even though the opportunity had arisen several times. After everything he told her today, she even understood his compulsion to hide away in the desert. Torque's crooked smile swam before her eyes and once again, she decided to trust her instincts rather than her logic.

"Maybe I will show you my house. You can tell Torque how L.A. people live." His smile told her he was pleased she decided to trust him after all.

"See you in the morning, Donna." Tracey waved as she

strode past. "Thanks for taking care of Jann while I was gone."

Donna was busy on the phone, but waved as they headed out the front.

"Nice little girl." Jann grinned as he held Tracey's door open for her.

"Obviously, the feeling was mutual, Erikson. You'll have to park on the street, or in the beach parking lot across the street. We've only got one space per unit. Is that all right?"

"Sure. I'll manage."

"Okay. Stay right behind me, so you don't get lost," she warned. "I'll signal before I turn off."

They merged into the afternoon traffic that wound its way along the coast like an undulating reptile. The weather was pleasant and warm compared to the foggy days that had shrouded the beach towns last week.

Tracey rolled her window down partially, allowing the wind to tug at her hair. She monitored the rearview mirror and smiled at the big black Ferrari that filled her vision. Jann wore sunglasses, so she couldn't see his eyes, but she could see his wide grin in the shadow of his car's interior. Her stomach fluttered at the thought of bringing him into her home. She signaled to turn and waited for him to make his way into the public parking across the street.

The Jaguar swung elegantly into the small space reserved for its owner, then Tracey cut the power and alighted from the low-slung car. Jann had already crossed the street when Tracey reached the sidewalk to meet him.

"Nice place," Jann said, tucking his hands into his pockets. His gaze swept over the wrought-iron railing that barred her small patio from the sidewalk. From the outside, her condominium reminded him of similarly designed residences in southern Spain. A two-story structure, it had Spanish roof tiles and an arched stucco entryway. Like its owner, Jann determined, it had a cool, detached air about it, as if no one or nothing could penetrate its sophisticated exterior.

She produced a key which unlocked the gate to allow them into the courtyard. A second key unlocked the front door. Jann maintained a comfortable distance between them, but he could still smell her honey-scented shampoo, and feel the heat of her gaze.

"I wasn't expecting company," she explained as they entered the black-tiled foyer. "I really was ill, in spite of what Donna implied. There are dishes in the sink."

"I won't look in your sink," Jann promised, as he reached for her hand. He pulled her back against him and wrapped his arms around her. His heartbeat accelerated as the smell of her perfume wafted close. He felt her shiver as though frightened and wondered if she were.

"You're trembling. Don't be scared, Tracey," he whispered, turning her to face him. "I didn't come here expecting payment for anything I've done."

He felt Tracey relax against him. She turned, circled her arms around his neck, and hugged him. He had come to trust her more than he had anyone else for a long time.

"If I'd thought that . . . we wouldn't be here," she admitted, backing away. She slipped off her flats and carried them in one hand. "Come on." She held her free hand out to him. "I'll show you the rest of the house."

Jann noticed that beneath her stocking feet, her toenails were, indeed, polished.

Tall vertical blinds in the living room shaded it in a pale blue light, giving her furniture and fixtures a warm, homey atmosphere. They held hands as she led him up three short stairs into the hallway.

"The bathroom," she said, switching on the light.

Jann peered inside at the black sunken tub and patterned tile that wrapped around the spacious cubicle. A large beveled mirror filled the wall above the vanity and sink, brightly lit by dressing-room–style makeup lights. An exotic tropical plant lifted its arms toward the skylight and provided a separation between the tub and commode. In anyone else's home he would have expected to see a lady's shaver, a crumpled towel or nightie draped over a knob, but not in this room. Tracey kept her house as well ordered and tidy as she maintained her car and her clothes. "Um-hmm," Jann said, and followed her down the hall.

Tracey pulled the cords that drew the sheers back, exposing a mile-long length of beachfront panorama. Jann unlocked the glass doors and stepped onto the patio that was encircled by a wrought-iron railing. A circular stairway wound its way to the ground-floor deck he had seen from outside.

"Beautiful view."

Tracey slipped her arm around his waist and looked out over the ocean. A heavy sigh escaped her. "I like it."

"Pretty noisy," Jann observed. "I don't suppose it bothers you?"

They stepped back into the suite arm in arm.

"You get used to it. I just block it out." She pulled the sliding door closed, shutting out the noise, and drew the sheers across the view.

Her spacious bedroom reminded Jann of the many hotel rooms he'd occupied during his travels.

Back in the hall, Tracey moved toward him and grasped his outstretched hand. Slowly, he drew her into his arms.

Her kiss was shy, playful. She tasted cool and minty. He felt her smooth skin. His feelings for her were anything but playful.

Jann wanted to forget everything that stood in their way. She was beautiful, sensitive, romantic. It didn't matter that they were in L.A. They were together now. He reached around her, but felt her pull away.

"I'm sorry, Jann, I—" She stood. "I better change."

"I'll wait in the living room."

When he left her alone, Tracey placed both hands on her flaming cheeks. Her bedroom mirror confirmed her suspicion. She had brought a virtual stranger into her home. She had to be losing her mind. Her flushed face and darkened eyes told the story. How could she do such a thing if she weren't in love? Crazy. Mindless. Hopelessly in love. With a man who didn't share her feelings. It was absurd. And it was a first.

Men had always been interested in her, but she had never felt this way about them. *But he doesn't love you,* her mind reasoned. Tracey eyed her reflection reproachfully. *He does. He just doesn't know it yet,* she decided. *I'll have to take it slow. He's been hurt and it wouldn't take much to scare him away. Approach with caution.* Tracey envisioned a highway sign.

She removed her skirt and lifted the unbuttoned blouse over her head. *That's what I intend to do,* she thought. She pulled on tan-colored slacks and a knit T-shirt. *He's skittish, and will bolt at the first sign of encroachment,* she reasoned. A few quick strokes with the hairbrush restored her coiffure and composure. *Take it slow,* she resolved finally.

* * *

Jann looked over her home. He wandered over to an office portico next to the kitchen and eyed the certificates and awards on her wall. Her ambitions to not only *have* the best, but *be* the best were evidenced by numerous framed certificates of several achievements: one was a parchment scroll and a snapshot of her at what must have been her kindergarten graduation. Another showed valedictorian of UCLA School of Design, First Place Award for 1997 Interiors Showcase. Several ribbons and awards were displayed in a rectangular shadow box. Magna Cum Laude graduate of UCLA. He understood now that she was strong-willed, and competitive. And from what he had learned from her, she had set her sights on winning the Death Valley Dilemma.

Jann walked over to the living room fireplace, picked up a miniature terra-cotta dog from the mantel, and inspected it. When she reappeared downstairs, he met her gaze then returned the figurine to its resting place.

"Mayan," she explained. "Would you like to sit down?" She indicated the couch.

Jann's brow lifted, but he sat without answering. Tracey seated herself on the arm, placing a good distance between them.

"Well?" she asked.

Her rooms were meticulous and it appeared to Jann that she kept her condo in model-home condition. It was tasteful, uptown, and except for her personal awards wall, sterile, he decided.

"It's nice," he said, his voice empty, polite. "But—"

"But what?"

"Is it you?"

"What do you mean?"

"Everything's perfect," he said, settling himself into the

deep cushions of her white, circular couch. "Too perfect." He ran his hand over the rough woven fabric of the cushions. "It doesn't feel like anyone lives here. It looks like you transported Taos into Santa Monica."

Tracey frowned.

"I like it, don't get me wrong, but is it really you, or the look of the '90s?"

"Of course it's me. I chose every bit of this—the drapes, the furniture, the accessories."

"It belongs in the desert, not in Santa Monica," he insisted.

"It belongs where people enjoy it. Who says because I live in the East that I have to collect period furniture? Or because I live in L.A. I have to like contemporary and abstracts? And how does a man like you who surrounds himself with apple crates, a waterbed, and a big-screen TV, think he can pass judgment on someone who doesn't?"

"It proves to me what I've known all along, Tracey. You're hung up on how things look to everyone else. I doubt you took a whole lot of consideration in what Tracey Evans, the woman, wanted. Take that print." He pointed at the large metal-framed Gorman that hung on the north wall. "Do you actually have a feeling for that woman holding the basket? Or did you buy it because it matched the decor? Did it remind you of someone you knew? Or someone you'd like to know? What about that candleholder? Is it functional? It looks like you've never used it."

Jann stood and looked around the room for more evidence. "What about the little dog? What does it mean to you? It's Mayan. I'll bet it doesn't mean a thing. It's there because it looks good. Am I right?"

His question had validity, Tracey admitted to herself. But what was he really saying? Was he criticizing her because she hadn't met his expectations? Maybe that was behind his disapproval, but he was treading on thin ice where her decorating was concerned. This was her livelihood. Her life.

Tracey was shocked at how incensed he had become. Maybe she didn't know him as well as she'd thought. She cursed her lack of judgment about inviting him into her home. He was agitated and she felt more than a little uncomfortable.

"Am I right, Tracey?" he repeated.

Tracey was afraid, but his singular attack on her character was something she would not tolerate. Without weighing the ramifications further, she retaliated.

"You have a lot of nerve lecturing me about appearances, Jann Almighty Erikson. You couldn't wait to barge into my life, flashing that Ferrari in front of Donna—showing off who and what you were. And what about those tires? Pirellis? Why not good old American Dunlops or Goodyear, or Sears radials for that matter? You had to have the best. I would have settled for something I could afford, but you had to have the most expensive set on the road. And you're calling my house a showpiece?"

"My choice was based on quality, Tracey, not prestige."

"Call it what you want, but it's no different than what you just accused me of. And if you're quite through tearing me and my life apart, I'd like you to leave. I'm sorry you bothered about the tires. If I had my old ones back I'd take yours off, but it looks like I'm stuck with them. You can order another set and I'll float a loan to pay for these."

The stark silence stunned her when she realized they had been shouting. Tracey raised her chin, marched toward the door, and yanked it open. "Please leave, Jann. Now."

Jann held his head erect. "I'm right, you know."

"Three seconds." Her hand gripping the doorknob, she stood sentrylike.

"I'm sorry," Jann muttered. "I didn't mean to—"

"Don't say it, Jann. You've been kind, but I think you've got some problems to sort out that have nothing to do with the way I decorate my house. You may have recovered physically from the accident, but—"

"Like you said, keep your opinions to yourself. And keep the tires. Let's just say I can afford to throw them away." Angrily, he brushed past her.

Tracey locked the door behind him then bounded upstairs to lock the sliding glass door. She stood at the edge of her drapes and watched as he lunged into the Ferrari and sped out of the parking lot. She flung herself on the bed, muffling her sobs with a pillow.

After work on Friday, Tracey met Lynn for her manicure appointment. It didn't take long to fill her friend in on the events of the past week. Pain heavy in her heart, she relayed the incident at her condo before Jann had left. Tears stood in her eyes and she wiped at them with her free hand. Lynn studied her friend wide-eyed from beneath a shock of orange-tinted hair with blue-tipped bangs.

"You mean to tell me—"

Tracey nodded her head, affirming Lynn's assessment.

"Well," she huffed. "I'd tell that sorry son-of-an-Erikson where he could take his opinions."

Tracey sighed, reflecting on the incident. "I thought I was over it, but it still hurts. He was so vicious. I mean, I took him into my home and he—"

"You're lucky he didn't do worse than that," Lynn scolded. "What in the world were you thinking about, bringing a stranger into your home?"

"He wasn't really a stranger, Lynn. We'd been together several times and he acted—"

"Like a maniac," Lynn declared.

"It's not really his fault," Tracey conceded. "After what he went through I can understand his feelings. But, it's like the accident warped his perceptions. He's rejected what's normal as bad. I can almost believe I'd feel the same way if that had happened to me."

"Sounds like you're defending him, girlfriend."

"Maybe I am. He's right about my place, you know. Santa Fe, adobe, and weavings are in right now, and I like them, but they're not really me."

"Well, then what is?" Lynn asked, shaking her large hooped earrings as she patted the nail polish in her palm. "You want the same color as mine tonight?"

Tracey eyed the bronze metallic polish Lynn held up and sighed. "No, I think I'll go with midnight blue—it matches my mood."

"This might cheer you up," Lynn encouraged.

"Oh, I don't know what I want, Lynn. All I know is, a bright light has gone out of my life." Tracey felt a familiar ache in her heart that lodged in her throat. Tears blurred her vision. "It's like I opened a door and peeked inside, then someone slammed it shut."

"Sounds to me like that flu you had affected your brain, Tracey. Are you sure you're up to that race?"

"Of course I'm sure. And you better be, too," Tracey reiterated. "It's just you and me against Al Brack, and we're going to take the trophy from him this year."

"Right," Lynn cheered. "One week from tonight. I'll be ready."

As the day of the race drew closer, Tracey became more uneasy and irritable, as if Jann's foreboding words might have held a valid concern. She wished they hadn't parted on such negative terms. Still, she hadn't instigated or deserved such an unwarranted verbal attack. She was not the one to blame for what had taken place. She hoped she would do well in the race, and put an end to Jann's unnatural distaste for her competitive instinct.

When she returned to her condo on Thursday evening the phone was ringing as she opened the door. Tracey dropped her purse on the floor, left her keys dangling in the lock, and ran to answer it.

"Tracey . . . ?" a familiar but strained voice croaked.

"Yes? Who is it?"

"Lynn."

Static jarred the line as Tracey struggled to listen.

"You're not going to believe this, but I've got a raging fever, a cough, and a bathroom I can't stay close enough to."

"Oh no, Lynn. You couldn't. You didn't. What happened?"

"I think it's the flu."

Chapter Eight

It was well after midnight and still Tracey lay wide-eyed and awake in her large bed. The nearly full moon shone bright through the clerestory windows above the sheers, reflecting on the inky black ocean. Her room echoed with the sound of waves as they reached the shore.

For the first time since she'd joined SCCA, Tracey would be a no-show at a rally. This, after all she'd been through. She had depleted her savings to pay Jann for the tires and for other mechanically related expenses she had incurred for the Jaguar over the past month. Not to mention the entry fee and reservations. The rooms were paid for in advance, and she'd only get a token refund if she didn't participate.

"I've got to race," she told her cat. "I can't give up now."

Again, she mentally reviewed people who might be candidates for the dubious position she offered.

Her mother? No, she wouldn't drive over fifty-five.

Her brother? Ohio. Too far away. Donna volunteered once, but now she had a hot date. And stodgy Merle? She could just see him in his pseudo safari jacket, hanging onto the door handle, waiting for her to land for the last time.

No one in her circle of friends was willing or able. It was possible another driver had lost a navigator, but that would mean one of them wouldn't be able to drive. The rules were clear and very strict—one navigator and one driver per team, positions not to be shared or altered after the race began.

That left the one man whom she couldn't dare ask under the circumstances—Jann. He, of all people, would be the first one to refuse. Hadn't he tried to discourage her all along? Hadn't he warned her about the risk and the danger? About the reality of losing life and limb? Ask him to navigate? *I must really be mad,* she concluded.

Morning dawned in a pearlescent beauty. The luminous moon of the night before was still in evidence as it hung in the morning sky. The ocean, with ever-changing hues, was tinted a silvery gray, edged with lacy ruffles of foam.

Rasputin began his daily dance, begging to be released outside, and Tracey heard the familiar chug of the automatic coffeemaker as it brewed.

She checked her face in the mirror and thought she had never looked more forlorn. Suddenly she remembered the prints of sad-looking, large-eyed waifs that once hung in her teenage bedroom. *I wonder where those pictures are? I liked them once. Would they be in my room now, if they matched the decor?* She studied her face intently looking for answers that refused to come.

Filled with frustrations, Tracey's day dragged. The patterned curtains she had ordered to match a client's wallpaper, were off a shade. A carpet had accidentally been rerouted to St. Louis; the factory that shipped it didn't have another roll in stock, and Tracey had promised delivery by Monday at the latest. It had to be the worst day of her life.

By noon, she felt tired, hungry, and devastated. Months in advance, she had scheduled her afternoon off, so she'd have time to pack and dress for the weekend. Time forced her hand, and she either had to phone Jann, or the rally-master and forfeit her fee. Lynn would pronounce her crazy. Her mother would disapprove. Jann would probably hang up on her before she had a chance to ask. Brack would laugh all the way to the winner's circle.

It took two more cups of coffee to bolster herself, before Tracey assembled the courage to call Jann's shop in Inyokern. Anxious, Tracey held the phone to her ear and paced in her small kitchen, waiting for an answer. After the seventh ring, finally the line clicked and Torque answered the telephone.

"Hello-o-o," he drawled.

That probably meant Jann was out of town, she guessed. Either that or out to lunch.

"Torque, it's Tracey."

"Well I'll be. I woulda bet silver dollars to snakes you'd give us a holler. How are ya, little lady?"

"Pretty good, Torque, but I've got a problem. Is Jann there?"

"He's in the back gettin' a bite to eat. What's the matter? You sound about as low as the belly on a sidewinder."

Tracey felt her courage sinking along with the disappointed tone of her voice. "Everything," she answered. "I lost my navigator."

"Is that somethin' like a compass on that jig-a-jag?"

"Kind of," Tracey lamented.

"Well, let me get Jann to the phone. He'll be right glad

to hear from ya. He's been moping 'round here like a pup that lost its playmate. Hold on jes' a minute.''

Tracey heard Torque call his friend to the phone by saying, ''Jann, there's some woman on the phone wants to talk with you.''

At least Torque hadn't written her off. For that, Tracey was grateful. She braced herself and held the handset tighter against her ear, wondering if Torque would let him know it was she who called.

Jann took his time getting to the office phone, but when he finally answered, Tracey summoned all the salesmanship she possessed to pitch her offer.

''Jann, I know we've had our differences, and you left on unfriendly terms, but I . . .'' Her voice faltered.

''Tracey?''

''Yes.''

''What's the problem?''

''The race.'' Her stomach twisted into knots, but she rallied herself quickly.

''What about it?''

She decided to try Torque's approach and shoot straight from the hip.

''Lynn is sick and if I don't have a navigator, I'll have to forfeit.''

After a long silence on the other end of the line, Tracey continued. ''I know how you feel about racing, and I understand the reasons why, but is there any chance you'd consider helping me out? All your work and my money is tied up in this thing and—''

She paused. She heard nothing in the earphone. No static. No dial tone. No breathing. ''Are you there? Jann?''

''I'm here.''

She wondered what to do next. Obviously she had made a mistake.

"You probably don't have the time. Don't worry, Jann. It was just a thought. I understand. Really."

"What time is it?"

"About two o'clock." Tracey answered.

"I mean the race. What time does it start?"

"You mean you'll do it?"

"When does it start?" he repeated.

"Tonight. Eight o'clock. We're supposed to meet at Dirty Sox Wells."

"That gives me about six hours." He paused. "I'll need a set of British standard tools and a couple of things you might need. You better leave a little early so I can look the engine over before we take off. I'll have Torque fill in for me while I'm gone. My place, six o'clock," he clipped.

Tracey's mouth dropped as she held the dead phone in her hand. All she heard was the steady tone that signaled he had hung up.

"He's going," she murmured, hanging up the phone. "He's going." Her voice rose to a triumphant shout. "Rasputin . . . he's going to race with me!" She squealed and leaped in the air, sending the surprised cat scurrying for cover. "You sweet little cat."

Tracey picked up the disgruntled animal and stroked its soft fur on her cheek. "You be good while I'm gone. I won't be back till Monday."

She set the feline down and hurried toward the bedroom, talking to herself. "I can't believe he's going to do it."

As she gathered things to pack, Tracey checked it off a list she had prepared weeks ago. When it came to choosing sleepwear, she halted. It hadn't occurred to her before now, but she would be sharing a room with Jann.

"Oh no." She groaned. "What have I done?" She tried to remember what the rally brochure had to say about the room accommodations, but decided there would probably be two beds in each room, so they could work things out. *Jann is a gentleman, as far as I know,* she thought, trying to convince that voice in her head that always reasoned in the negative.

After she had taken care of Rasputin's needs, she backed the car out of the carport on her way toward Inyokern.

Three and a half hours later, Tracey pulled the final hill before turning off toward the town Jann called home. It was even smaller than she had remembered. Had it only been three weeks ago?

She leaned toward her rearview mirror and stole a glimpse of her reflection one last time before they would meet. Her hands moistened, making a mockery of her cool facade. She resisted wiping them on her thighs where they'd leave a mark on the cotton flight suit she had chosen for her driving attire.

The sun had already begun its descent in preparation for night when Tracey left the highway for the narrow strip of road that led to Jann's garage. After she pulled up, a lone figure emerged from the darkened shop, carrying a weekend bag and an armful of gear. For a moment she didn't recognize him, until Jann stood beside her window and motioned for her to roll it down.

"You're running late, Ace," he said, without the usual courtesies. "Open the door so I can stash this stuff."

Tracey's reactions were as sharp as his voice. He seemed brusque and businesslike, which suited her just fine. Maybe they wouldn't have the camaraderie they had enjoyed prior to his L.A. visit, but if it meant avoiding a scene like the last, Tracey preferred it that way.

She reached across the passenger's seat and flipped the lever that opened the door.

"You're different. What did you do to yourself?" she asked.

"Not much. How 'bout you? How've you been?"

Silence was her answer as their gazes met in the dim interior light.

"Pop the hood," he ordered. "I'll check the water and oil before we take off."

When he was through, he left the shop for the last time, carrying a wad of clean rags that he stowed beneath his seat.

"Let's go."

He shut his door and strapped himself in.

Tracey wheeled away from the glowing green light in front of his garage.

"This way." Jann pointed north toward an access road. "It's a shortcut. I test-drive my cars out here."

Tracey drove away from the town and made her way into the growing darkness. When she got a good look at Jann she realized not only had he gotten his hair cut, but he had shaved his beard as well. His clothes were crisp and new, and he smelled of shampoo and cologne.

"You look nice," Tracey said, wanting to feel the smooth skin of his face in her hands.

Her resolve to maintain an emotional distance from this enigmatic man was dashed. He appealed more to her now than he ever had. She didn't know how she had managed to get through the week without knowing she would see him again.

"I missed you," Jann said, echoing her thoughts as he touched the back of her neck.

He eyed her clothing, marveling how she could turn

something so simple into such a stunning outfit. A wide leather belt, that looked as soft as the skin at her nape, gathered the waist of the suit into a narrow fit. He wondered how she could breathe. He sure as heck couldn't. The thin fabric draped over her contours, not hiding the fullness beneath. Beige button earrings hid the lobes of her ears that he knew to be soft and sensitive. She wore her hair piled on her head, held in place by several combs. Tracey had twisted a hand-printed cotton scarf around her neck and wore it knotted at the base of her throat.

He had driven himself crazy this past week, wondering if he'd ever see her again. It was hard being so close now, not being able to hold her as he wanted. To feel her in his arms again.

He had never yearned for a woman—or waited for one—as he had with Tracey. But he had to give it more time. He was on board as a navigator, and he knew that was all she wanted or expected from him. Anything more, and she'd call the whole thing quits. Thinking about her was a bittersweet torture he had to call to a halt. He removed his hand from the back of her neck and shifted his weight forward.

Tracey squirmed in her seat as she tried to keep her eyes focused on the road ahead. *I hope he's not reading my thoughts,* she mused. Forcing her concentration back to the race was not as easy as enjoying the company of the man beside her. It was more difficult trying to ignore him, now that he was right here with her, than when she tried to block his presence from her thoughts when he was two hundred miles away.

She longed to rake her fingers through his thick wavy hair. She wondered how his face would feel, newly shaven as it was, against her neck. She strayed onto the shoulder of the road as her thoughts removed her from the present.

"Hey," Jann cautioned.

Steering the Jaguar back into her lane, Tracey shook her head of fantasies.

"Sorry, Jann. I was daydreaming."

He laughed in a low, husky tone and patted her hand. "That's okay. I've been a little distracted myself."

Tracey felt her cheeks burn, then she smiled at her passenger.

"Thanks for coming, Jann. You can't imagine what this means to me."

"Sure I can," he said, settling in his seat. "It might be best if you don't introduce me to the others, though. I'll try to be the invisible man."

"Why?"

"Might make 'em nervous, that's all."

"Someone might recognize you," Tracey stated, beginning to feel worried. "Do you think I need to inform the rallymaster that I switched navigators? I didn't think that'd be a problem."

"Well, if anyone thinks they know me, I'll just act 'like I ain't never seen a Jaguar before,' " he teased, switching his voice into Torque's hillbilly drawl.

Tracey giggled. "It worked on me once. I know you could pull it off."

Outside of Olancha, the now-full moon had begun its ascent at the crest of Coyote Peak and slowly rose in all its iridescent glory. The air smelled like rotten eggs. Or as Jann informed Tracey, "Mineral springs."

As they drove into the starting checkpoint at Dirty Sox Wells, most of the others had already assembled in front of the makeshift podium. The rallymaster, J. C. Brandsen, a stocky, no-nonsense senior with a voice like thunder, called the group together with a booming command.

"Let's head it up now, folks. You've got a long way to go tonight, and we're going to get started on time. Has everyone checked in that you know of? Carl, what have you got on your ledger?"

A thin, balding man wearing metal-rimmed glasses stepped forward, studying the paper on his clipboard.

"Let's see," his high nasal voice whined. "I've got two no-shows, one cancellation, and I was told Taylor and Taylor are on their way."

"Okay," Brandsen addressed his audience again. "For those of you who haven't entered one of our SCCA-sponsored races before, we have a few items that need to be pointed out."

He drew forth a handbook that was flagged in several spots and read specific rules of conduct outlined by the national board. As he wrapped up his speech, a late-model Corvette pulled in and Taylor and Taylor, a husband-and-wife team, scrambled from the car.

"As you know," Brandsen elaborated, "you will receive a sealed set of instructions for each leg. This packet is not to be opened until you have been flagged out of the starting gate. If at any time, our crew determines that these instructions have been opened, the seal broken or tampered with, you will be disqualified for that leg. Every leg counts to the total number of points in your class, then against the highest accumulation of points overall. Any serious breach of etiquette will not be tolerated, and the perpetrator will be heavily penalized, fined, or disqualified. Do I make myself clear?"

A resounding volley of affirmations responded.

"Now, I need a volunteer from each team to take shifts

guarding the vehicles. We have not had any vandalism in the past, but it has been our practice to rotate guards throughout the night to prevent any incidents. Check with Carl for your time slot, either Friday or Saturday night.

"The first cars out will be Class F, the novice class in the four-cylinder category. Ready, Carl?"

Carl read a list of seven names from his ledger, and asked the entrants to form a group to one side.

"Those people whose names have just been called may come up for their first set of instructions. The rest of you will be called up in your class groups, and the first car out will leave precisely at eight o'clock. I'll be available for any complaints, comments, and general goodwill throughout the rally, and I look forward to seeing you at the victory banquet on Sunday night. Good luck, ladies and gentlemen, and Godspeed."

A boisterous cheer rose from the crowd as Brandsen stepped down, giving the spotlight to Carl. "Class E. . . ."

Tracey looked around the milling contestants' faces and sought out the one who had plagued her in past events. At Soda Springs, the last event, Tracey had managed to come closer to Al Brack's nearly perfect score than anyone else in their class. She found Al in the rear, a cigar clenched in his gold-capped teeth. His navigator was a new man Tracey didn't recognize, but one whom she didn't think she'd easily forget. His hair was slicked back like a fifties tough, and he sported a blue satin racing jacket with the Marvin Jaguar logo on the shoulders. Brack hadn't changed since Tracey had seen him at the Soda Springs rally in the fall. He still wore that cat-in-the-cream grin that made her feel as if he thought everyone else was an inferior being.

"That the man?" Jann asked, nodding his head in Brack's direction.

"Yeah," Tracey answered. "The smug one with the cigar in his face. I don't know his sidekick, though."

Jann eyed their opponents and looked thoughtful for a moment. "I do. That's a pit-crew punk named Richie Lange. He used to work for a NASCAR friend of mine, but he let him go. He was a good wrench, but my friend seemed to think he had sticky fingers. . . ."

"You mean he's a thie—"

"Uh-huh," Jann whispered. "You can bet he knows me, too."

As if the two men had heard their conversation, they both looked in Tracey's direction. She smiled thinly and turned away in time to see Jann duck into the crowd.

Chapter Nine

When her name was called, Tracey stepped forward and accepted her packet of instructions. She and Jann would be racing in Class E, novice equipped. Her fingers tingled with excitement as she headed toward her car. Jann waited inside the Jaguar, "maintaining a low profile," as he put it.

The cars in her class were to be the last flagged out that evening. Four other classes, A through D, were already well into Death Valley Dilemma. Jann's quiet presence made her feel warm and secure. She had a sense of command with him at her side.

As they waited their turn, in the dim light she could make out the features he had, until tonight, kept disguised behind his beard. Now, the Nordic influence was even more discernible as the slight angle of his cheekbones and solid jawline were exposed, ending in a squared, stubborn chin. His hazel eyes were hooded beneath smooth auburn brows.

"Like it?" Jann asked, grinning.

"Yes." Embarrassed that he'd caught her looking, Tracey answered, "You look good."

She continued her study. "There's something different about you, though, not just your appearance."

Jann shifted in his seat. "I didn't think you'd notice."

"What did you do?"

Jann cleared his throat and sighed. "I've, uh—been doing a lot of thinking. And seeing a therapist." His admission didn't come easily. Tracey felt his awkwardness but tried not to let her own discomfort show.

"I thought about what you said. You were right. I had let the accident color my judgment. It dictated everything, my actions, my outlook. This is the first time in years I haven't carried the weight of Armand's death on my shoulders." He trained his gaze on her. "I just didn't know it showed."

Tracey met his gaze with understanding. "They say a man either cuts his beard or lets it grow when he undergoes a personality change. I guess it's true."

He chuckled and self-consciously tugged the corner of his mustache. "Well, I'm not ready to shave this yet." Then his facial expression grew serious. "I've got a long way to go, Tracey," he said, covering her hand with his. "But thank you. I feel better."

"On the contrary, I'm glad you agreed to help me out. I was so afraid to ask. I couldn't sleep all night."

"I'm here for selfish reasons of my own," Jann confessed.

Tracey's stomach flip-flopped. She hoped he wasn't feeling the same pull of attraction that she was. If he was, they wouldn't be able to get through this race at all.

"Like?"

"I never thought I'd race again. Even though this is

nothing like what I used to do, it's still a race. It still incites the same apprehension, excitement, tension, fear. I still have nightmares about the accident, and it scares me. I knew eventually I'd have to face the monster I created. I'm here to see if I can.''

Tracey breathed a sigh of relief, then searched his eyes for the emotions he must be feeling. For him to admit he was frightened was bold. She felt sure Jann had begun the healing process. That she had been able to contribute toward that bent pleased her.

Jann laid the packet on a lighted clipboard. ''Ready?''

''Ready,'' she repeated.

She smiled, feeling bonded to him. They were about to embark on a trip that would no doubt see them through a myriad of emotions from start to finish—a mini partnership in a capsulated time period. Where their relationship would go was beyond her scope of vision. But maybe it was destiny that had brought them together to begin with. Maybe . . .

The checkpoint crew waved Tracey forward. She started her engine and joined the line of Class E cars that formed at the entrance to the campground. When she stopped at the gate, the big six-cylinder engine vibrated under her hands. The car had never been more ready for a race, and Tracey felt more confident than she had at any other event.

Jann seemed to be taking it all in stride. He appeared nonchalant and detached from the excitement that charged the air. The team manning the starting gate asked for the instruction packet, inspected it, then handed it back to Tracey through the open window. Her number forty-four was adhered to the driver's door and right front corner of the bonnet in six-inch-high numerals. All of the cars had been checked out and equipment approved prior to starting, so now they were down to the wire.

A crewman raised a green flag, all the while eyeing the large stopwatch he held in his hand, then he and his partner began the countdown. "Four, three, two, one—Out."

Tracey tromped the pedal and felt gravel spray from beneath the rear tires as she sped from the starting gate. Jann opened the envelope with his finger and drew out a piece of paper. The sheet he unfolded was a computerized printout of instructions that he read aloud.

"Leave gate at 35 m.p.h., 1.3 miles. Increase speed to 48 m.p.h. 8.7 miles then cruise 35 miles at 55 m.p.h."

"I'm coming up on 1.3, Jann."

"Prepare to increase speed to 48."

Tracey listened to the rhythmic clicking of her tripodometer, as it measured the distance she traveled in hundredths of miles. The smooth-running engine emitted power to her hands.

In front of them, the full moon had risen higher, mirroring its reflection on the long, sloping nose of the Jaguar. The desert looked pale outside, dotted with dark clumps of sagebrush; the sky a translucent indigo blue. The only wind that rushed by was created by the big machine that cut through the air. A low-voltage interior light positioned over the tripodometer illuminated the compartment, so they could keep an accurate record of time, distance, and speed throughout the rally.

Jann read through the instructions to determine where they would stop that night.

"Stove Pipe Wells," he said, grinning. "That's where we'll end up."

"Is that good or bad?" Tracey wanted to know.

"They've got a wonderful pool." Jann's face held an amused expression. "Maybe I'll take a swim later on."

"It'll be after midnight when we get there, won't it?"

"Yeah. I'll probably sleep like a baby after that," he teased. "What's your distance?"

"Coming up on 7.9."

"Prepare to increase speed to 55."

Tracey was pleased that Jann seemed to be taking the event seriously, as if it mattered to him as well. But according to what he told her, he was only involved to the extent that it served his purposes. He would help her follow instructions to the best of his ability.

"Eight point seven," Tracey called.

"Increase speed to 55."

Their first checkpoint was at Panamint Springs. As they pulled alongside the rally staff, Tracey rolled her window down. Jann studied the notebook she had brought along, keeping his face obscured. The crewman logged their time then knelt beside the car.

"We've had reports of burros on the road, so be alert. We don't want any accidents tonight."

The crewman and his partner set their stopwatches, started their countdown chant, then waved her on. "Out!"

Shortly after takeoff, the instructions directed her to make a sharp right-hand turn heading south. The moon shifted positions as they made the turn, now bathing Tracey's left side in the bright light. Jann looked at his partner's profile, a shimmering halo of spun silver/gold framing her face.

"I guess I didn't tell you earlier, but you look nice, too."

"Thank you, Jann." She smiled, then added, "Don't think I'm too dressed up, huh?"

He chuckled. "No, you look fine. But I still like the way you looked wrapped in that sheet."

"Erikson, did anyone ever tell you you're a male chauvinist—"

"Red-blooded American?" Jann winked at her. "What's your distance?"

Tracey checked her odometer and gave him the figure.

"Good. It's perfect with the trip. . . . Your boys in Santa Monica install that for you?"

Tracey nodded. It wasn't a fancy odometer, but it was accurate, and that was all that mattered. "They've put in a few of them for our members. There are four of us in this event. The two Mark Twos in D Class, the Austin Healy mini-coupe in Class A, and mine."

"This is kinda fun," he decided. "I've never competed on this scale before. It feels good." Jann looked out his window to the flat, low valley they drove through.

Pleased, Tracey smiled. This might prove to be good therapy for him. She hadn't counted on that. "You know where we are?" Tracey asked.

"Yep. We'll pass a dirt-road turnoff soon, Slate Range Road, then according to this sheet, we'll turn left, heading northeast past Rogers Peak. Remember Wildrose Canyon?"

"I think so."

"We drove through it when you were here."

"Oh, yeah." Tracey recalled the narrow, steep road that snaked above the canyon and wound into the Panamint Valley.

"We'll be driving through there. I know for a fact there are burros in that area because of the spring. So, be careful."

"What do I do if they're on the road?" she asked. "Do I honk, or what?"

"Just don't hit 'em."

"Right." She grunted. "As if I'd drive my Jaguar through a herd of burros."

"Mark," Jann stated, using a racer's term for "what's your distance?"

"49.5."

"Stand by . . . next instruction . . . prepare to make a left turn, reduce speed to 35 m.p.h. . . ."

After their second checkpoint at Nemo Crest, another series of curves and hills led them to a graded dirt road, which they were instructed to follow at a speed of 15 m.p.h.

"This used to be Harrisburg," Jann told her. "We're over a mile high, did you know that?"

"Really? What in the world were people doing out here?"

"Mining. Gold, copper, you name it."

"Like Torque?"

"I guess so."

Tracey envisioned the isolation of the mining town, set high above the rolling plains of barren wasteland, and the desperation of the people who sought it out, risking all for the elusive strike. People like Torque and Tilly. They must have had a hard life.

"So what's Torque up to?" Tracey asked.

"Minding the shop. He said he'd stick by that phone in case that 'Jaggy war' of yours broke down."

Tracey groaned and shook her head. "Let's hope not. No offense, Jann, but I hope I never see your tow truck again."

He laughed. "You don't like my truck?"

She frowned at him, but he understood. If the car was

incapacitated to the point of needing a tow truck, she'd be out of luck. And out of the race.

The dirt road circled back onto the main paved highway and they continued their ride north. At midnight, Tracey saw lights in the distance, from what she supposed was their final destination.

"Is that it?"

"Yep. Stove Pipe Wells. They'll have a buffet or something set out, right?"

"Probably."

She pulled into the final stop where the checkpoint crew waited with flashlights and notepads.

"Good timing, Ms. Evans," the crewman congratulated her.

"Thanks."

"We're setting up the first watch in fifteen minutes. No one will be allowed in the parking area until tomorrow, so be sure to remove anything you might need for the evening."

Tracey nodded and drove her car to the edge of the makeshift parking area and shut it down. She cocked her head and listened to the creaks and ticks of noise from the engine as fluid settled in the lines. Gratefully, she heard nothing worthy of alarm.

After driving all evening with Jann less than an elbow apart from her, now she was getting nervous. He hadn't asked about the sleeping arrangements, and she hadn't brought it up. Tracey reached for her bags and pulled them from the back. Jann removed a shaving kit from his leather bag, grabbed his blanket, then locked his side of the car.

"You think you'll need that?" Tracey asked.

"I told you, I never go anywhere without it."

"You're not bringing any clothes?"

"What for? I haven't gotten these dirty yet." He extended his arm to help her. "Want me to carry one of those?"

Before she could respond, he had removed the strap from her shoulder and transferred it to his own.

"I'll wait while you check us in," he said. "And stay out of the crowd for a while."

Tracey adjusted her purse on her arm and marched to the registration desk. The clerk checked off names and handed out keys since the rooms had been preassigned and prepaid.

When it was Tracey's turn to be helped, she said, "Evans." The clerk ran her finger down the list of names until she reached Evans. "Evans and Morris?" she asked, seeking clarification.

"Uh, yes . . ." Tracey hedged. "That's right."

"Here you are." The gray-haired woman smiled. "Enjoy your evening."

"Uh, excuse me . . . but, are there two beds in the room?"

"Why, no, miss. Most are one queen to a room. Unless you requested two singles, that's all we have."

The woman must have read concern in Tracey's face as she suggested, "I've got a rollaway if you'd like to use it."

Al Brack sidled up to the counter and leered. "My partner and I are roomin' solo, Tracey. You can bunk with me if your navigator needs his rest. That is, if you don't mind consorting with the enemy."

Tracey rallied a halfhearted smile.

"Thanks, Al, but we'll manage just fine."

She took the key, thanked the clerk, then checked the room number. Tracey wouldn't give Al the satisfaction of knowing what her relationship with Jann was. To leave him guessing was to her advantage at the moment.

Tracey headed through the portico toward their room. Out of the shadows, Jann emerged and touched her elbow.

"Jann . . ." She gasped. "You scared me."

"You're jumpy."

"I, uh, guess I am a little tense. The driving and all."

"Have anything to do with Brack?"

"No. Come on. Let's find the room and grab something to eat. I'm hungry."

They walked through the stone colonnade where others had already seated themselves at the patio tables and chairs. A poolside buffet table had been set up, and the majority of the people were still in line. Underwater lights illuminated the pool, inviting guests for an evening swim.

"I gather you've been here before?" Tracey asked, wondering if it had been in the company of a female.

"Yeah. If I remember correctly the water is solar-heated and it's real nice. So . . . where's our room?"

The smile on Jann's face heated Tracey from her knees to her neck as she pondered her next move. "Jann, there's a bit of a problem. . . ."

His brows raised, waiting for her explanation. "I do have a room, don't I?"

"Well, yes, of course, but I didn't know I'd be sharing it with you and—"

She stopped in front of their room and met his questioning gaze with her own.

He held out his hand, and Tracey laid the brass key in the middle of his opened palm. Jann fitted the key in the lock and looked around the tiny bedroom. It was as he remembered the place—quaint, rustic, and it housed a single queen-sized bed.

"A little smaller than my king," he remarked.

Because the hotel was unique, in that it catered to occasional visitors and not the mainstream tourist crowd, Tracey guessed that most of the rooms offered the same accommodations. She could see he was enjoying himself, but she wondered if he was thinking about the problem.

"I wondered if all the rooms were decorated the same," he rambled. "I like the log beams and the flagstone floors, don't you?"

"What about the bed, Jann?" Tracey asked, hoping he'd have a reasonable solution.

"When I was here before it was real comfortable. Not as soft as my waterbed of course, but—"

"There's only one," Tracey pointed out.

Jann's grin was unbearably smug, Tracey decided. She wasn't going to resolve this problem with his help, that was evident. She didn't know how she could ask the clerk to move a rollaway in without the whole world knowing about it. And apparently Jann didn't think it was necessary.

I asked for it, she decided. *Every bit of this.* Having him navigate was hard enough, but it might prove to be the easiest part of this trip. No woman in her right mind would have asked a man to do this.

Jann assessed Tracey's expression and determined she'd been teased enough. She looked miserable sitting in the wide-armed easy chair that filled a corner of the room. He was in love with Tracey. He knew that now. Those days and nights without her had been more than he could bear. If she hadn't called, he would have, begging her forgiveness. He was wrong about her. She was a beauty all right. Inside and out.

"Don't worry, Tracey. I'm just kidding you. I've got my trusty blanket, remember? I'll just bunk on the floor, or even outside. You're the driver—you take the bed. I'm not going to jeopardize your race by keeping you up all night. Let's get some food before it's all gone.''

They locked the door and walked through the open hallway where the buffet was laid out. It was a lovely, calm night, and the temperature was pleasant, mild. Some of the guests had already decided to enjoy the pool, as they dived in and splashed in the water. Tracey edged her way to the buffet and garnered a plate for herself and Jann.

She caught Al Brack and his navigator staring. Fortunately Jann stood with his back facing them. Maybe they hadn't gotten a good look.

"Jann," she whispered. "Al and that Lange guy are watching us."

"So? Let 'em watch."

"What if they recognize you? I didn't tell the rallymaster I had switched partners."

Her stomach lurched as Al and his cohort moved their way. Panic seized her and she felt her heart pounding.

"They're coming over, Jann. What'll we do?"

"Nothing. There shouldn't be a problem."

Tracey thought he sounded too sure of himself in a situation where maybe he wasn't the authority. As they approached, Jann took matters in his own hands.

"You've got enough there, don't you?"

Tracey eyed the piece of ham and single celery stalk she'd acquired, before Jann took the plate from her, set it down on an empty table, and whisked her in his arms.

"Let's dance."

Tracey complied, hoping it would spare her from the unpleasant confrontation she expected with Brack. They joined others already dancing to the soothing lyrics that poured from the outdoor speaker, as Jann guided them in that direction. Jann swept her into the shadows near the other end of the pool. He nuzzled her face with his and inhaled the scent in her hair as they swayed to the romantic strains of a slow song.

He reached for the decorative clasp that held her hair up, and tried to free it.

"What are you doing?" she asked, covering his hand.

"Taking your hair down," he whispered. "I like it that way."

He clasped his hands at her waist, not letting her go, while she reached behind her head and pulled the combs that held her hair in place. She shook it loose and let it brush her shoulders as it swung free.

"That's more like it," Jann whispered, pulling her closer to him.

She tried to maintain the appearance of decorum although Jann had maneuvered her into a difficult position.

Tracey peeked at their opponents, who still watched them from a distance. She saw the younger man scowl as they talked, then they turned and retreated to the lobby. It seemed as if Jann's idea worked.

"They're gone, Jann. You can let go now."

"Um-hmm," he murmured.

"Did you hear me? I said they're gone."

"Let's finish this song first," Jann coaxed. "I've never danced poolside under a Death Valley sky before. It feels good, doesn't it?"

For a moment she held onto her rigidness until he ran his hand lightly from her neck to her waist and back again. With the tingling, she let her feelings flow with the music as she moved with Jann. She'd like nothing better than to stay in his arms forever. . . .

"Jann?" Tracey whispered.

"Mmmm?"

His throaty response filled her with a longing that coursed deep within her soul and sparked a fire there. She couldn't deny her feelings, but she had to control them. It wouldn't be fair to either of them to fall in love. They would both end up being hurt. They were, after all, only weekend partners and when the race was through, they'd be living separate lives again.

The song ended and Tracey moved out of his arms. His face looked soft, illuminated from the patio lights, and she could see the heavy-lidded look that told her how he felt.

"Shall we finish dinner?" Jann asked, not releasing her.

Tracey nodded.

They walked hand-in-hand back to the table where their food lay waiting. The buffet table was nearly empty, and the crowd had thinned to a few couples who seemed as content as Jann did to be outside. They ate in silence, then Tracey swirled a swizzle stick in her coffee, mixing cream with the ebony liquid.

"Tired?" Jann asked, caressing her hand.

"Surprisingly, no." She looked at the moon that had risen and begun its pre-morning descent on the western sky. "I hope I feel the same way in the morning when it's time to get up."

Jann chuckled. "It's nice out here. I'm going to change and take that dip I was talking about. How about you? Want to join me?"

Tracey hadn't given it serious consideration before now, but it didn't seem like too bad an idea.

"We're supposed to guard the cars at four A.M. O-o-o-oh." She groaned. "How are we going to manage that?"

"You brought an alarm clock, didn't you?"

"Yes. But if we went to sleep right now, we'd probably

get only three hours at the most, and that's sleeping an hour after we got off watch.''

"If you work it right," Jann suggested, "you can get by on a couple of hours' sleep. We did it all the time. You just have to get in the right frame of mind. And make sure you get plenty of sleep the next night," he added.

They quickly changed; Tracey occupied the bathroom while Jann used the bedroom for their individual dressing rooms. The large stone archway opened onto the pool and patio area. The place was deserted when they returned. It seemed everyone else had the good sense to turn in for the night.

Jann tossed his blanket onto a lounge chair, followed that with his towel, then dived in off the side. Tracey dipped her foot in first, then splashed her leg in the water.

"Oh, it *is* warm. It feels wonderful."

She dived in, then bobbed up next to Jann who was treading water in the middle of the pool.

"I knew you'd like it," Jann said, smiling.

Tracey frolicked in the pool like an otter in a pond. The water invigorated her and she swam several freestyle lengths before pausing to rest at the side of the pool near Jann.

Hanging onto the ledge for support, he circled his arm around her waist and drew her to him. Water droplets clung to her thick lashes, cheeks, and chin. The water shimmered and danced from the underwater lights.

Tracey ran her fingertips over Jann's cheeks and chin and traced the line of his lips. He nipped at her finger and she drew it back and laughed. He was teasing her again.

She questioned her giving herself up to the enjoyment of being with him. She had just recovered from the flu, she'd had a stressful week, and she was tired after driving several hours. She didn't trust her ability to think straight in a weakened state.

As if he knew her thoughts, Jann deliberately broke their contact. He paddled backward, forcing distance between them.

Tracey's eyes felt as large as the moon overhead. She had done it again. It seemed as if she had no will when it came to Jann. He only had to be close enough to kiss and she was a goner.

"Had enough?" he asked.

"What?" Tracey asked, stunned.

"Swimming," Jann clarified. "Had enough?"

His mischievous grin could not be disguised by the innocent look he tried to project. "You're right." She hoped he was giving her an out. "We better turn in."

Jann's head remained motionless as he treaded water. "I'm going to hang out here a while and swim a few laps. You go ahead."

Tracey placed both palms on the rock ledge, then heaved herself up, twisting as she went, to sit on the side. She kicked her feet back and forth, allowing the water to soothe the muscles that had been cramped in the car all day. She swung her legs up and over the pool's edge and snatched her towel. Draping it over her shoulders, she patted her face dry, blotting her hair as she headed toward their room. If she hurried, she would be able to shower before he would join her.

Jann watched as she left the lighted pool area and slipped into the shadows of the stone portico. She was everything he'd hoped for in a woman—intelligent, gentle, ambitious, good-looking. And she was a looker, all right. She was the kind of woman who would draw a man's eye whether she was wearing blue jeans or a bathing suit, he mused. But especially in a bathing suit.

He swam several laps, then cooled down with a relaxing breaststroke. When he saw that Tracey had turned the main light off, he drew himself from the water, and sat on the side dangling his feet in the pool. In only two hours, he would stand their watch.

Jann silently entered the bedroom and took a quick shower. Tracey was breathing deeply and had already fallen asleep. He watched her for a moment, and resisted the compulsion to stroke his hand on her cheek. The alarm clock had been set for 3:45. He pushed the button off and slipped from the room, back into the desert night, where he made his bed on a reclining deck chair.

The sound of a key jiggling in the lock woke Tracey. She sat upright and stared bleary-eyed as Jann walked through the door. Golden shafts of light streamed in from behind him.

"Good morning, sleepyhead," he said, as he crossed the few steps to her bed.

His hair was wet and he was barechested and barefooted, a white hotel towel draped over his neck.

"Where have you been? Swimming?"

"I swam a few laps after the four o'clock watch. I was in the kitchen talking the cook out of a cup of coffee." He raised a stoneware mug as evidence.

"You didn't wake me up," she accused. "I was going to stand watch, too."

She checked the clock then smoothed her hand over her tangled hair. She felt vulnerable under his steadied gaze and wished he hadn't caught her in disarray.

"They only asked for one person per team, and you need to be in top form for the drive."

Jann sat down beside her on the bed then leaned toward her and kissed her lightly on the lips.

"You look lovely," he said.

His gaze roamed her face. His husky voice sent shivers rushing over her skin, where dewlike droplets from his hair fell onto her face and neck. Tracey's stomach fluttered and she drew the sheet higher to her chin.

"Want some?" he asked, offering her the mug.

"Thanks." She took the cup, sipped the warm brew, then handed it back to him.

"Did you stay out all night?"

"I slept by the pool and swam after I got off watch, so I'm sure if I was noticed, it certainly wouldn't arouse curiosity."

He rose from the bed and shoved the cup into her hands.

"I'm going to get a shower, while you get dressed."

"Go ahead." Tracey grinned. "I had mine last night." She sobered. "And Jann? Thanks . . . for everything."

Jann shut the door behind him.

"I know, I'm a great guy," he shouted over the running water.

Chapter Ten

The air buzzed with chatter from the rally contestants and crew. From novice to old-timers, energy ran high as the breakfast buffet ended and the rally hour closed in. Tracey balanced two cups of coffee and napkin-wrapped pastries in her hands. She and Jann strolled outside the hotel's perimeter to escape the noise and notice.

Distant mountains were a pristine picture of varying shades of blue, violet, and pale rose tints, warmed by the unobstructed sun. The air was still, filled with the early-morning peace that the desert shares with no other clime. Sagebrush, bottle-green in the pale light, released its pungent odor in the tremulous breeze. Her professional instincts on target, Tracey looked back at the desert inn with an interior decorator's view.

"You know, Jann, I've been thinking . . ."

"That can get you into a lot of trouble, Ace."

"I've wanted to make a change for some time, but I was afraid."

"Of what?"

"Failure. As long as I'm working for someone else, I'm not fully responsible for the outcome. I've got an out."

"So you do want to strike out on your own, or you don't?"

"I've thought about it a lot. But I'm not sure I'm ready for it."

"What about the Bakersfield branch? Didn't you say they're looking for a senior designer?"

"Yes. I could work with them for a while. See if it's feasible to take over. It would give me time to get a good feel for running it on my own."

"That sounds reasonable. Low risk," he added.

"We've been talking about doing a magazine feature. I could work with the Bakersfield staff on it. I wonder if the owners of this inn would let me use their lobby."

"What are you getting at?"

Tracey hesitated as she gauged his reaction.

"I thought if you wanted to . . . give our . . ."

"Relationship?"

"I don't really like that word. I was thinking more of—"

"Companionship? Partnership?"

"Well, you know. Get to know each other better."

Tracey glanced at Jann and saw him smiling.

"Bakersfield is far enough away—"

"One hour."

"I could lease out my condo, lease one in Bakersfield. I wouldn't be sitting on your doorstep, and it's close enough that we could spend a lot of time together. If you want to, of course."

"Of course." He grinned.

"What do you think?"

Jann tilted his head and Tracey could see his facial expression was thoughtful as he stared into the desert. Jann's ideas of "getting to know each other better" might be a little more direct than Tracey's.

"It wouldn't hurt to try," Jann admitted. "Your Taos tastes would fit right in here, wouldn't they?"

Tracey shot a warning side-glance at him.

"You know, I never apologized for—"

Tracey interrupted, "Forget it, Jann. You've more than made up for any indiscretions. I shouldn't have blown up myself. Besides . . . you were right. That's probably why I reacted so badly."

Jann's expression conveyed his surprise.

"I admit my tastes do run with the trend. That doesn't mean it's bad, but I understand how people can lose sight of who they really are. In my business I need to keep that in mind."

"Well, that's what I tried to say. I just didn't know how to say it."

"You've been invaluable to me. I wouldn't be able to race now if it weren't for you."

"Well, it looks like the competition is a little stiff."

"I know. I'd give anything to wipe that smirk off Al Brack's face. Just once. I know I can beat him."

"He's got Lange," Jann mused, "but then, you've got me."

"Do you suppose they've discovered who you are?"

"I didn't run into them last night, but I wouldn't be surprised if Lange has figured it out. Not that it matters. In a way it might be good."

"What do you mean?" Tracey asked.

"It might make your opponent nervous if he thinks I've been giving you driving lessons."

Tracey groaned. After Jann's dancing demonstration last night, and their escapade in the pool, she was sure Brack and his partner were convinced driving lessons weren't the only reason she and Jann were together.

"Looks like they're ready," Jann said, looking over the crowd that had begun to form near the cars. "We better get moving."

Tracey tried to quell the nervous flutter in her stomach as she walked toward the dirt parking area. Brandsen was in good voice this morning as he relayed last-minute instructions to the drivers. While Jann returned to the hotel room to gather their things, Tracey made her way into the crowd. She smelled the odious cigar before she saw Brack.

"Your boyfriend's got quite a reputation, Evans. You sure know how to pick 'em."

Behind her she heard Al Brack's nasal laughter mingle with another male voice. She turned and looked straight into the cold, calculating face of Richard Lange, who stood next to Al. The mean expression in Lange's eyes chilled Tracey even though she was fully exposed in the sunlight.

"Think you've got a chance this time?" Al challenged, forming his words around the cigar he held in his moist lips.

"As good as anyone," Tracey countered. "You might be surprised."

Al's chuckle sounded like a toy gun firing staccato noise instead of bullets. "Not this time, luv. You'll have to do better than Jann Erikson to beat me."

Lange and Brack moved away, leaving her verbally wounded and trembling with determination.

"Remember." Brandsen's voice reverberated in the still

air. "We are all gentlemen and ladies, and no matter how badly you want to win, fair play is of utmost importance."

"Are you listening, Brack?" Tracey muttered.

"What's that?" Jann asked, taking his place at her side.

"Watch your back," Tracey cautioned. "Brack and his slippery sidekick are on to you."

"We'll have to be extra careful where you park your car," he cautioned. "It wouldn't take much for Lange to disable it. A well-placed nail, sand in the gas tank . . ."

Tracey's eyes rounded. "He wouldn't—"

"I wouldn't put it past him. Men like that have no scruples where a race is concerned. I ought to know."

Clapping hands signaled the end of Brandsen's speech. Bolstered by Jann's presence, Tracey allowed him to guide her toward the car. Parked near the back row, the Jaguar's chrome gleamed in the unfiltered sunlight, acting like mirrors as it reflected the brilliant rays.

Tracey unlocked the driver's door then released the lever from inside to allow Jann entry. As before, the cars from Class A, B, C, and D drove out ahead, then the Class E cars lined up in the preassigned order.

She was amazed at how attractive Jann looked. He had showered and shaved and his burnished hair glistened in the sunshine, waving lightly over his ears and collar. The cologne she had grown to love filled the compartment with its leathery scent and reminded her of their drive to Mt. Whitney. To Tracey, eons had passed; she felt a lot older, but just a little wiser.

When she pulled up to the starting line, Tracey received her instructions. She counted down with the crew, then sped away, leaving a cloud of dust in her wake. The tripodometer began ticking with the first turn of the wheel, developing its own musical pattern as Tracey accelerated.

Ripping open the envelope, Jann called out the designated speed, then quickly read through the instructions and interpreted their commands.

"You're good at this," Tracey complimented her partner, while focusing her eyes on the road.

"Yeah, well . . . I guess it comes easy when you've been in the line of work I used to be in."

"Look, Jann." Tracey pointed. "Burros!"

A group of white-eyed miniature donkeys stood like pensive sentinels about thirty feet from the road on the side of a hill. Their dusky black bodies looked sturdy and well fed even though they grazed on the sparse pickings from the open range.

"Not a very big herd," Jann commented.

"Do you think we'll see more? They sure are tame little beasts."

"Probably will. Although the government's been giving 'em away all over the States, I'll bet there are plenty left in the valley."

They drove a series of timed legs that morning and found themselves headed for Scotty's Castle Monument by noon. Tracey motored the cocoa-colored Jaguar over the top of a hill, then gasped in amazement at the large stone castle that emerged in a guarded area of rocky hills. Red clay tile adorned the roof in precise layers. A watchtower, crowned with an American flag, rose from among a cluster of buildings that resembled a medieval Spanish fortress. She was awed by the beauty of this hidden oasis as they drove past a swimming-pool moat and crossed over the bridge to park with the others in a fenced area.

"What a fantastic place to live! I can't wait to see the inside!"

Jann smiled, prompted by the pure joy Tracey exuded.

He liked the way her hair was tied back from her face and pulled to one side. She wore cotton khaki slacks and a white military-style blouse with epaulets on the shoulders. She looked casual yet sophisticated with her sunglasses hiding the sparkle in the gray eyes he had come to love.

"I think they're serving lunch," Jann said, pointing toward a stand of salt pine trees. "Maybe we'll have time to tour it when we're through," he suggested.

"I hope so. I'd love to see the interior. Whose is this, anyway?"

"National Park Service owns it now. An Illinois millionaire hooked up with a local miner named Scotty. They became friends and Scotty brought him out here and took on the position of contractor. It's fabulous inside. German craftsmen paneled the rooms with wood from the Black Forest, Spanish tile and chandeliers imported from Spain— well, you get the picture."

"Out here?" Tracey asked, incredulous.

"The man was ill. The weather back East wasn't good for his condition. He came out here to be alone and recuperate."

Tracey's gaze swept across the spacious grounds. "It's just beautiful. I can understand why he'd want to live here."

"Like me?"

"His idea of 'hiding out' was a lot more grandiose than yours, Erikson."

Jann unbuckled his seat belt, got out, and locked his door. "Come on, if we can't see it today," he coaxed, "I'll bring you back."

Lunch was served on a verandah that overlooked the grounds, adjacent to the apartments where park service employees were housed. From her vantage point, Tracey could see her Jaguar and felt confident all was well. The rally team catered lunch, so it was a simple fare of sandwiches, salad, and fruit, with plenty of iced canned pop. Several rallyists meandered the concretcd estate, or rested under the shade of palm and Joshua trees. Oleanders bloomed in profusion and shared their heady scent with the breeze that carried it on its back. After their four-hour drive that morning, Tracey and Jann rested and stretched their legs, preparing for the remainder of the afternoon.

At one o'clock, the first cars in A class were on the road. Class E would leave about thirty minutes later. The checkpoint crew was helpful and courteous. It made the rally smooth-going and pleasant for all concerned. Camaraderie between the contestants grew, except for the egotistical Al Brack. His offensive tone could be heard over the crowd's, no matter where they stopped or for how long. He and Lange acted like bullies in a schoolyard, intimidating and mocking those whose cars did not equal the horsepower of his Marvin-sponsored Jaguar.

New instructions for the upcoming leg indicated a complex combination of speeds varying from ten to fifty-five miles per hour that ended in an afternoon break at Artist Palette. The Palette was a checkpoint with a built-in downtime that afforded a breathtaking view of a unique desert vista. Mountains in the foreground looked to be millions of years old, never inhabited by man or animal. Like its name, the area was a veritable palette of richly hued colors winding in delicate, variegated patterns of turquoise, violet, cream, and rose.

The warm afternoon sun radiated heat from the pavement, emitting waves of air in layers above the parched earth. After a brief respite, a new set of instructions were given and they were on their way. Jann could see they were

leaving the national park and heading south, probably toward Las Vegas. The directions indicated long stretches of
straight roads at speeds that allowed the driver to push it
to the max.

"Mark your distance," Jann ordered.

As the afternoon wore on, Tracey's eyes felt strained
from the dry air, the bright reflection of the sun from the
unprotected landscape, and too little sleep. Her movements
became mechanical, as she clasped both hands on the steering wheel and downshifted only in the curves. Other rallyists dotted the road in the distance, looking like slot cars
on a child's toy track.

Suddenly, the car's engine raced, but it was losing momentum. Tracey lifted her foot from the pedal and slowed
the car, veering toward the side of the pavement.

"What's happening?"

Jann grasped the wheel for any indication of tire problems, but felt none.

"Pull off slowly," he directed. "You're doing fine."

They broke from the pavement and eased onto the hard-
packed shoulder. A flapping noise from the engine slowed
then stopped when Tracey cut the power.

"Pull the release lever, quick." Jann sprang into action.
He unsnapped his seat belt and flipped the bonnet lever in
lightning speed. He reached for the tools he had brought
along. Together they raised the bonnet.

"What is it?" Fear rose like bile in Tracey's throat.

"Threw a belt."

She peered down the road at the maroon-colored Jaguar
that grew larger as it neared. It roared up in a jet stream of
heat, showering sand pebbles onto the downed car. Al
blasted his horn as they passed. Tracey saw the laughing

face of Richard Lange and imagined Al's look of pure delight as they sped by, pointing at their opponent.

"How long will it take?" she asked, hoping she hadn't blown the leg. Every precious second added to the weight of impending failure.

"Not too long. Think you can catch that bird?"

"You mean those vultures?" Tension tied knots in her stomach. "Of course."

"Good."

Jann reached in and tested the other belts for tightness. "Looks like you're set." Pressing a gentle hand to the bonnet, he guided it down to where it latched.

"Lock this down. Let's hit it."

Tracey felt she had a chance to make up the four precious minutes she had lost, aware that had it not been for Jann, she would still be struggling with that belt. She knew enough about the car to get by, but couldn't act quickly in crisis situations. Replacing a thrown belt in the middle of a race would have been just that. She offered a silent thank-you to the universe for sending the calamities that had thrown Jann and her together again. A cloud of dust and sand plumed upward as she spun the Pirellis out of the dirt and back onto the road.

The final checkpoint was situated outside of Las Vegas, and they were given directions to the glamorous high-rise that would be their resting place for the evening. Dinner was an "on your own" affair that allowed the contestants an evening of show-hopping or gambling at the casinos of their choice.

In their room, after she had unpacked a few things and set her cosmetics out, Tracey called for room service and had their dinners brought to them, to avoid the others. Jann laid claim to the double bed by the window, and Tracey was relieved to see a generous amount of space separated the two beds. He wasn't very talkative after they had eaten.

Tracey tuned in the local news. Jann seemed happy. She heard him whistling in the shower with the spray gushing full force. Trying to concentrate on the weather report, Tracey turned the television volume up to drown out Jann's tune. A seasonal storm was moving in off the coast in an easterly direction.

"Heavy showers are expected mid-to-late afternoon in the desert regions," the weatherman warned, circling the vast area of desert that encompassed California, Nevada, Arizona, and southern Utah. About that time, a commercial ended the report and Jann emerged, faded jeans riding low on his hips. Smelling of hotel soap and his cologne, he stood wiping water from his hair.

She smiled. Her heart fluttered, keeping time with the tingling sensation that ran through her stomach.

Jann's towel hung from his shoulders as he moved toward Tracey and pulled her into his arms. His lips were soft, his kiss gentle. His clean, moist skin felt warm and inviting.

Tracey succumbed to the pressure of his kiss, sweeter than she remembered. He had been so patient and kind all along, she mused, from the time that he had first towed her car. But he also had the strength and magnetism of a raw, red-blooded male.

"You going to shower?" Jann whispered, nuzzling her hair.

She backed away feeling self-conscious and confused. She didn't know how long she could maintain the emotional distance their relationship required. Taking her night-clothes with her, Tracey cloistered herself in the bathroom and ran a full, hot tub. She emptied a portion of her shampoo bottle under the faucet and created a fragrant bubble bath to soak in. Feeling giddy, she eased herself into the water that moved up to her neck and wrapped her in a blanket of iridescent foam.

She heard the TV from the other room. Jann was waiting for her to emerge. *You're in over your head,* her cautious voice warned. She would have to stand her ground, Tracey decided. Take it slowly.

Chapter Eleven

Tracey pushed herself from the tub and toweled her smooth skin dry. She donned her pajamas and robe, then flung the door open.

"Jann—"

He lay with his back to her, half covered by his sheet. He wore his jeans and his breathing was slow and steady.

She crept closer and whispered, "Jann?"

He was asleep. A smile creased her face and she shook her head, relieved. She turned off the television with the remote control that was anchored to the nightstand. Then, pulling her covers down, she slipped in between her own crisp sheets, reached for the moveable lamp above her head, and switched off the light.

The phone alarm rang, jarring Tracey awake. Heavy floral-patterned drapes disguised the dawn and she focused her eyes on the hotel's digital clock/radio. Six A.M. Jann stirred.

164

"On your feet and into the dead of the heat," he mumbled a well-worn racing verse.

"Hi, Jann." Tracey smiled, dangling her feet over the edge of her bed.

"Who's first . . . you or me?" he asked, his voice garbled with sleep.

"Me. I'm already up and halfway decent." She chuckled, checking her pajama top for unsecured buttons.

"Just my luck," he muttered, watching her exit.

He walked to the window and drew the thick curtain aside to look at the world below. Their room was on the twenty-third floor. People and cars looked as if they were part of a museum's moving display. The view was magnificent from their vantage point, facing the mountains to the east that encircled the desert Mecca. A few fingers of gray clouds reached over the horizon toward the sunrise.

"Looks like we might get rain," Jann shouted.

"That's what I heard," she answered, as she emerged from the bathroom.

If Jann had learned nothing else about Tracey this weekend, he had learned she didn't rely on much in the way of artificial enhancements. Her hair always smelled of the rich honey-scent shampoo she used, and she applied a minimum of makeup. She didn't have to work at attracting a man. She was a natural.

Although he hadn't believed it at first, Tracey's appearance was not an act. For her, looking polished and well groomed was a state of being. She had an air of sophistication about her that was not put on.

She managed to appear "put-together" no matter what she wore. Today she had dressed in the same slacks, but topped it with a peacock-blue sweater that clung attractively to her rounded contours.

Jann's breath caught and he murmured "I'm glad this race is almost over. You've done more damage to my will-power than I was prepared to handle."

Tracey met his appreciative gaze with one of her own.

"Your turn in the bathroom, Erikson." She planted a kiss on his nose then breezed past him to take a look at the clouds herself.

The sky did seem gray this morning, and she'd bet that on the western side, storm clouds would be in evidence.

The first car left at eight o'clock, and Tracey waited beside the Jaguar for Jann. He had gone back to the restaurant to have his coffee thermos filled. She spied Al and his slick-haired shadow with a circle of men and their girlfriends, evidently sharing a joke. Al's loud guffaw stiffened Tracey's spine, and she watched as Lange left the group and headed her way.

"Where's the famous Mr. X?" he asked, when he'd gotten into speaking range.

Tracey didn't like the look of his beady dark eyes that raked her body like an offending claw. She folded her arms across her chest.

"He's coming."

"Brack's going to let you run the race, then pull the plug out on you and your buddy," he sneered.

"What do you mean?"

"You'll see."

Lange wasn't aware of Jann until he approached him from behind and tapped him on the shoulder.

"Hello, Lange."

"Well, if it isn't the Grand Prix goon," Lange taunted. "How's the wing? You got it all healed up?"

Tracey stood wide-eyed and shocked. She studied Jann's face and observed his balled fists unwind.

"Gotta go, kids," Lange bleated. "See you at the banquet tonight." He hunched his shoulders to the wind and joined his loud-mouthed friend.

Jann covered his left hand with his perfect right one and rubbed it gently.

"You all right?" Tracey asked. "I'm sorry he said what he did."

"*You* can't be sorry for what someone else has done," Jann clipped.

He removed the thermos from under his arm and shoved it inside the car. "Pull the latch, will you? I want to check the fluid levels."

Jann seemed uneasy throughout the morning's runs, but Tracey had no reason to believe it was anything she had done. Rather, she surmised, it had been Lange's viciousness that had gotten to him. She wondered if the impending storm had set Jann's memory in motion.

All morning, they drove beneath an overcast sky through North Las Vegas and into the Valley of Fire to Logandale and Arrow Canyon.

They were about to embark on the last portion of the race—one that was designed to give everyone a final opportunity to make up for times lost, and errors made. The "speed run," aptly named, allowed drivers to make up for any downtimes by shaving minutes off the allotted timeframe. Tracey had lost two and a half precious minutes overall yesterday, and she hoped to make that up today.

If the participants are like me, she decided, *they are all tired, grumpy, and ready to end the race.* The weather added to the gloominess she felt. She hoped the storm would pass. But that was not to be.

The storm broke after lunch as the rallyists returned to their cars. Wind and rain slathered the thirsty desert with torrential force. Some contestants had brought slickers and hats. Tracey always carried an umbrella, but hadn't unpacked her jacket. Adding to her worries, Jann looked miserable and preoccupied. She leaned over and pecked his cheek. He was probably feeling as pensive as she was, she guessed, wishing the race were over.

The rally crew scrambled to organize the contestants, but the storm seemed to have upset everyone's equilibrium. Tracey heard shouts and doors slamming as people, pelted by rain, dived for cover in their cars.

As she buckled in, Jann muttered, "Take it easy, Tracey. These roads are like ice when they're wet. You'll have a hard time controlling a slide."

They moved up to take their place behind the others in Class E. Tracey could see Al in her rearview mirror, chewing his cigar and grinning at the same time. She shifted her eyes forward and pulled into the lineup.

As she revved the engine, Jann squeezed her hand. "Good luck."

His eyes looked clouded and far away. She imagined that somehow the rainstorm had set the wheels of pain turning. Would anything she could say ease his depression?

"We'll be back in the hotel sooner than you think," she said, trying to sound cheery. "And with any luck, we'll beat 'cigar-face' this time."

The crew huddled beneath a large umbrella and shouted to be heard above the noise. Tracey saw the green flag shoot down, and her thoughts converged into one objective. Speed.

Jann guided her south, toward what appeared to be the center of the storm. Ominous black clouds steepled to gargantuan proportions in the sky, looking like celestial skyscrapers.

Tracey recalled Brand's cautions at their pre-race briefing. "The rain might get nasty, so be extra cautious. Highway patrolmen issue tickets to rallyists the same as the general public. If you get caught, that's the risk you take. We do not encourage you to break the law, but to use your discretion about exceeding the speed limit on a restricted basis."

It was his official way of saying, "Do it if you can or must, but don't get caught."

The wet roads were less than forgiving to high-speed traffic. Jann remained silent except for the occasional interruptions when he asked Tracey to mark her distance and they synchronized speed to distance. The instructions led them through Piute Valley to Needles, where they crossed into Arizona. The rain-drenched landscape was devoid of vegetation other than the endless sagebrush and low-growing cacti.

As they drove toward Bullhead City, a fierce wind blew and the sky churned black, drenching the desert in yet another cloudburst.

Tracey's trio of British wipers slapped back and forth, but held no power against the unearthly downpour. She reduced her speed to a crawling thirty-five miles per hour as they wound around the curving road past Davis Dam. Until they reached Highway 93, Jann seemed tense and remained silent. At Kingman, they headed north on the final leg.

"It's a straight shot from here," said Jann, his voice barely audible above the overworked wipers. "We're down an extra five minutes. Better step on it."

Tracey followed his advice and tried to dodge the ruts in the road where cars had worn deep grooves under the desert sun. The lane was slippery and threw her car from side to side when she accidentally edged out of the asphalt slot.

"Careful," Jann cautioned. His mind slipped back in time. He saw himself in France. No longer a passenger on board the Jaguar, he was driving, harder than he should, making up time lost through the burgs of southern France.

Blinding lights of an oncoming vehicle shocked Jann back to the present. A gigantic truck and trailer headed straight for them in their lane. The truck's horn sounded as loud as a freight train. Tracey swerved to avoid their being crushed by tires that stood higher than the top of her car.

Her back tires gave way, as the nose-heavy car swayed. "Oh no, baby . . . Hang on."

They had already entered a skid. The front tires jumped the groove and pushed the car into the oncoming lane and safety. Tracey corrected the slide by oversteering to the right, but water stood deep on the road. Their speed sent them into an irretrievable spin.

It happened so fast, she was unable to respond to the forces that controlled the car.

Jann braced himself for impact. Softly, he instructed, "Hold the wheel steady. When you feel traction on the back wheels, steer into the skid."

Tracey felt as if they were on a "tilt-a-whirl" at a county fair, as her head and stomach experienced each 360-degree turn. Jann remained rigid and calm throughout. She felt the car reach the side of the road. She continued turning so they would not swing off the edge into the gully that paralleled the highway. Finally they lurched to a stop.

Jann's face appeared white within the darkened cockpit and slowly a smile formed. "You did it, Tracey. You pulled us through." He reached over as far as the seat belt would stretch and cradled her head on his chest. "You were great. You handled it like a pro."

As the adrenaline rush that had sustained her through the emergency subsided, Tracey's body trembled. "I'm shaking so badly I can't hold the wheel."

"You'll be all right," he soothed. "It's all right. It's over. Can you drive?"

"I think so."

"Are you sure?"

"Yeah!"

"Come on, Evans, let's win that race!"

Tracey whipped the car around, pointing it north, and tromped the pedal. If nothing else transpired that day, Tracey had mastered a spin that could have spelled death for a novice. She and Jann had done it. They were a team.

Jann urged her on. She ignored the grooves that tossed the car, as she shot forward through the slackening storm. Rain turned to mist then back to a hazy, gray sky. The storm had passed.

"Mark!" Jann called out.

"268," Tracey answered.

"Twenty more miles, Ace. Go for it."

She nudged the accelerator forward until the car reached a speed of eighty miles per hour. "How much time do we have to make up?"

Jann punched buttons on his hand-held calculator, then said, "You've got twenty-one point four minutes to do this next twenty miles. If you hold it at eighty miles per hour, we can make up six minutes and ten seconds."

Eighty miles per hour. Tracey did some figuring of her own. "In a sixty-five zone, that's at least a fifty-dollar fine, Erikson."

She met his smiling face with hers and floored the pedal.

The Jaguar shot through the damp air as if it were back on its native turf in England. The engine sounded tight, forceful and strong.

"That'll give you a handicap of eleven minutes, forty seconds if you keep this up."

"No problem."

As they crested a low hill, she saw a cluster of people standing alongside the road. Tracey slowed the car so she could stop if necessary. She recognized the Taylor and Taylor Corvette team. In front of them, Al Brack's XKE lay on its side. All four seemed unharmed and as Tracey pulled up, the Taylors waved her on.

Jann rolled down his window.

"They're okay," Mr. Taylor shouted. "Keep going."

Jann acknowledged the message with a "thumbs up." Tracey grabbed a lower gear and revved the engine.

Jann's eyebrow cocked upward.

She grinned. "I couldn't help myself." She increased her speed to over eight-five. "Just makin' up for that little delay," she explained.

A quarter mile down the road Tracey's attention shifted. The red spike on the oil pressure gauge darted erratically from side to side.

"Jann, what's this?"

He squinted at the instrument. "Looks like you're losing pressure."

"What does that mean?" Heat shot up her arms and hands. *Don't quit on me now.* "Is it serious?"

Jann's face grew reflective. "Could be. Let off the accelerator."

She did so and the needle dropped. A faint ticking could be heard in the engine compartment.

"Now accelerate," he ordered.

When she did, the needle jumped back to the middle, then jerked back and forth.

"What do you think?"

"Sounds like a rod, Ace."

"That's bad."

"Yeah."

"What are we going to do?"

"You've got two choices."

Tracey glanced at him.

"Either shut it down now while you've still got pressure and an engine, or . . ."

"We're so close, Jann. I couldn't—"

"Or, take your chances. It's your decision. It's the car or the race."

It had come to that. Tracey's heart pounded. She had risked everything so far, even their lives. But that didn't faze her like the possibility of burning up her engine. It was not only her sole transportation, but she loved that car. She wouldn't push it beyond its capability.

Her brow furrowed and she fought back tears. She checked the gauge once more. As she lowered her foot on the accelerator, the needle pulsated on normal. It dove down, then jumped back.

Jann reached over and squeezed her thigh. He knew there was a serious potential she would blow the engine. It had been a hard two-day drive. Seconds passed and the trip-odometer ticked loudly as the car ate up another mile.

"Twenty miles?" she asked.

Jann nodded. "Basically."

She pressed her foot further on the accelerator. "We're goin' for it."

Chapter Twelve

They made the checkpoint with a gain of five minutes, thirty-one point six seconds, which gave her a nearly perfect score. The race was over.

As soon as she could, Tracey pulled off the road. She hovered over Jann's shoulder while he inspected the engine for an obvious oil leak. He pulled the dipstick out and sniffed it.

"Rod bearing," he stated.

"Really?"

"Yeah. I can smell it. Here." He passed the dipstick beneath her nose. Tracey drew back. "It smells bad. I didn't hurt it too much, did I?"

"You can't drive it home."

"I know." She shook her head. "How far is L.A. from here?"

"About five hours," Jann calculated. "And about—"

"Five hundred dollars." Tracey guessed. "I'm going to

174

have to lay off the expense for a while and rethink the costs of this sport. It's set me back a lot more than I had ever anticipated.''

''I could call Torque,'' Jann suggested. ''I'm sure he'd—''

''No, Jann. I've imposed on you too much already. I'll just get a truck out of Las Vegas.''

''Suit yourself.'' Jann shrugged.

''I'll rent a car and drop you off tomorrow.''

''Let's get back to the hotel,'' Jann said. ''I think you can make it in all right.''

Despite the condition of her car, Tracey was consoled by the fact that Al Brack still waited for a tow truck to retrieve his Jaguar and had lost his coveted position.

Along with the race, Tracey knew their weekend had ended. All that remained were the scores, calculations, the judges, and the trophies. All events would be verified by the rally administrators, and the scores revealed at the victory banquet that night. But she knew how she and Jann had placed. He won back his heart. She had lost hers.

After they arrived at the hotel, Tracey had the concierge arrange to have a tow truck and rental car there in the morning. Then she and Jann took the elevator upstairs to change.

Tracey had brought one elegant gown, a simple design that was held at the shoulder by an oversized bow of the same expensive material. She showered, shampooed her hair, then blew it dry and brushed it until it shimmered in the mirror like sunlight dancing on a pond. She applied a dusky shade of green eyeshadow at the corner of her eyes that matched the color of her gown. She felt confident and proud. She and Jann had pulled together as a team to ride out that dangerous skid and emerged unscathed.

The uneasiness she had perceived from Jann earlier that day disappeared with the dark clouds that had swept through the Las Vegas valley. He whistled when she appeared from her makeshift dressing room.

"How do I look?" she asked, knowing from the expression on his face what he thought.

"There must be a constellation named after the most beautiful woman," he decided.

Tracey smiled. "Virgo represented the goddess of love, or mother goddess."

"You've got her beat, hands down," he said. "How about me?" He tugged at the corners of his leather jacket and turned to give her a full profile. "Will I pass inspection?"

"You look stunning, Jann."

He pulled her into his arms and held her.

"I couldn't have done it without you," she whispered.

"You did it all without me, Tracey, and you know it. All I did was keep the passenger's seat warm."

He cupped her head and held her against his shoulder.

"Jann?"

"Hmmmm?"

She met his longing gaze with one of her own, then lowering her lashes, she leaned into his kiss. When she opened her eyes, he was staring at her. His face was serene, yet a quiet strength radiated from within.

"You've shamed me, you know?" he said.

"How's that?"

"You're not anything like I thought you were. I was so wrong about you. I'm sorry."

"You had your reasons. Can't say I blame you, really."

"There's one thing you should know about yourself,

though,'' he said. ''You're a lot stronger than you think you are.''

''What do you mean?''

''You've convinced me there's *nothing* you can't do.''

''Like what? Drive a car?''

''Anything. If you give the same focus to your clients and your life the way you drive your car, you could manage your own business or Mason and Mignon's—north or south.''

''You really think so?''

''I'm sure of it.'' He nuzzled her neck. ''You've got more grit and character than most men.''

Tracey smiled. ''You're not just flattering me, are you, Jann?''

''How about you and I find one of those Las Vegas love chapels and get married?''

''Stop teasing me, Jann.''

''We can get hitched in the big city and spend our honeymoon underneath the stars. You can teach me the names of every one of them.''

''Get serious. You don't mean it.''

His expression became reflective and she watched the amber in his eyes deepen a shade. ''I want to tell you something, Tracey. I've done a lot of changing since I met you. You made me face myself.''

He released her and began pacing back and forth.

''The race. The accident. The years I spent trying to bury my feelings. I didn't tell you before, but I even visited a counselor after I saw you in L.A.'' He paused. ''I didn't know that my behavior was typical of people who've been through the same kind of trauma. Survivor guilt—and my hand. I thought it was just me.

''I feel years lighter. You've given my freedom to me.

I would never have done that on my own. And I wouldn't have willingly raced again either. But thanks to you, I did.

"When we spun out today, I was afraid we would die. I thought it fitting that I go the same way as Armand. I've carried the guilt of his death with me for a long time." Jann's voice wavered.

"It came clear to me when we stopped that I'd been given another chance to live. I was given the gift two years ago, but couldn't accept it. Today I realized what it meant. I'm not going to hide from life anymore. You've helped give it back to me." Jann's voice broke and she watched as the strong man buckled before her.

They bolstered each other as Tracey sniffed tears away and Jann leaned on her for support. Tracey lay her head into his shoulder and when his heart slowed its rapid beating, she whispered, "*You* did it, Jann. I'm glad I was with you when it happened."

"Stay with me, Tracey."

Her sigh was enveloped in his kiss as they came together.

"There's a lot more to consider than—"

"Are you going to take the Bakersfield position?"

His question made her realize he wasn't interested or willing to make their relationship any closer than the hour's distance that would separate them physically, or light years, emotionally. In spite of what he said, he made it plain. He wasn't ready.

"I'm thinking about it," she answered.

He kissed her softly, and they clung to each other as if to life.

"Do that, okay?"

"I will," she promised.

It was time to go. Reluctantly, she led Jann toward the elevators that would take them to the cocktail party that was in full swing. At seven o'clock, the banquet room opened. The other three couples in Tracey's Santa Monica chapter invited them to share their table.

Nervous chatter rose as more people gathered, until the room vibrated with the sound of a hundred voices all talking at once. Tracey trembled as she anticipated the moment she had been waiting for.

She and Jann toasted each other's success with a glass of champagne. The final hours of their partnership were coming to a close. Although exhausting, it had been a glorious forty-eight hours, and she hated to see it end.

The lines around Jann's eyes confirmed the strain he had undergone also. But he seemed content with the crowd, with himself, with her. They held hands. Without the self-consciousness he had exhibited before, Jann did not remove his scarred hand from hers. The amber lights in his eyes flickered and danced like the flame from the candle in their centerpiece.

When the judges seated themselves at the head table, she saw Al Brack and Lange approach the rallymaster. The two turned and pointed to where Tracey and Jann sat. Tracey felt color drain from her face.

"Darn," she whispered. "They've done it."

Jann's gaze followed hers to the front of the room, where the men conferred excitedly and looked their way. Al, rolling his rubbery cigar in his mouth, appeared as if he had gotten his wish. Tracey was sure he had asked that she be disqualified.

Dinners were served to the contestants, yet Tracey didn't feel like eating. Her stomach felt twisted and her mouth felt dry.

"Don't worry," Jann said. "You ran a fine race, and if nothing else, you can be proud of that. Everyone here knows what kind of times you were pulling. It's up to the judges now.''

Soon after eight o'clock, plates were cleared for coffee and dessert. The tension hadn't interfered with Jann's appetite, so he ate the chocolate mousse that Tracey couldn't touch.

When the awards presentation began, Brandsen stepped up to the microphone. ''I want to congratulate all of you for having survived Death Valley Dilemma. It proved to be the toughest race in our club history and tops any event other clubs have to offer. Even the weather had a hand in that.''

The audience responded loudly. Brandsen cleared his throat and continued. ''A complaint has been lodged against an E-Class individual for having brought a professional on board.''

It seemed to Tracey that the whole room leveled accusing eyes on her and her partner as the volume of chatter rose to a deafening roar. Tears gathered in her eyes, but Jann gave her hand a squeeze and she accepted her unwanted recognition with a defiant lift of her chin.

''Atta girl,'' Jann whispered.

''However,'' Brandsen continued, ''we are waiting for a ruling on this situation from national headquarters, so we will proceed, holding the final decision until the verdict has been reached. Now, on to the moment you've been waiting for.''

Polite applause heralded the beginning of the ceremony while Tracey accepted condolences from team members who shared her table. How Jann's former occupation would have affected her ability to drive the car didn't make sense to her. She leaned against Jann's shoulder and whispered, ''I'd feel bad if I were disqualified, but having you with me was worth it.'' She kissed his cheek and smiled at the auburn-haired man whose eyes held a loving glow.

After the other classes had received their trophies, all that remained was the trophy for Class E. The judges halted the awards while Brandsen left the table to accept his call from headquarters.

Brack wore the smile of a sadist about to begin some new horror on a victim as he left his group and approached the Santa Monica faction. Tracey's hands moistened, but Jann tightened his grip.

As Brack glowered above her, his gaze roamed lasciviously over the green fabric that complemented her feminine physique. His unwanted assessment caused Tracey's skin to crawl.

''Erikson, I didn't have a chance to speak to you earlier, but I wanted to congratulate you for all you've done for this little girl.''

''Oh?'' Erikson feigned mild interest in the other man's comment. ''What exactly was that, Brack?''

Al removed the wet cigar from his lips and laughed his maddening staccato laugh. ''Why . . . helping her with her 'driving lessons.' I'd thought of that myself.''

Embarrassment heated Tracey's face, but before she had time to react, Jann rose to his feet, towering above the offender.

Brack lurched backward and fell into the arms of a startled waiter bearing a large round platter of drinks. The two of them landed with a crash amidst shattering glassware. Red wine splattered over Brack's linen suit, giving it the look of a tie-dyed disaster.

The waiter scrambled to his feet and tried to help Brack up, while others from the hotel staff converged upon them. The episode took on the appearance of a Three-Stooges fiasco as Brack, spluttering and indignant, batted them away.

Brandsen returned to his position at the head of the table and beat a spoon on a plate to regain everyone's attention.

"Gentlemen and ladies, as I said before, there was a protest lodged we did not feel qualified to answer. I called the president of the National Board of the Sports Car Club of America, and after deliberating, he just returned my call. It is his opinion that because the nature of the professional's expertise was for driving, not navigating, and that he acted only in the navigating capacity, the member will not be disqualified and all events will be accepted as stands."

Tracey was shocked and elated. Apparently so were her peers as the room thundered with applause and whistling. It was with no small degree of satisfaction that she saw Brack and Lange arguing in the back of the room, surrounded by a bevy of well-meaning attendants still trying to clean the mess.

Brandsen motioned for the noise to cease and called the assembly to order. "It is my pleasure to congratulate a young member of our group who has shown tremendous growth not only in her racing expertise, but has managed to zero over ninety percent of the legs in this event. This same person and her navigator have earned the prestigious Gold Cup award for best team performance overall. Will Miss Tracey Evans and her navigator please step forward?"

Tracey leaned on Jann's arm for the strength it took to make that long walk to the front of the room. As more people recognized the man at her side, the noise volume increased, then exploded in a shower of cheering and waving. It seemed to her as if they were walking down a mile-long aisle by the time they reached Brandsen's outstretched hand.

Brandsen presented the race trophy to Jann, while Tracey

was awarded the Gold Cup. She held it above her head for all to see, but she focused on the smiling face of the man who helped make it possible.

After the banquet, many drifted into the dancing lounge, some pursued gambling interests, but Tracey and Jann strolled arm in arm back to their suite.

"Are you glad the race is over?" she asked.

"Glad it's over, and I'm glad you won. You did a great job. Are you happy?"

"I'm thrilled, of course. But I feel a little sad. Let down, I guess. I've put myself through so much this month— getting ready for the race, dealing with all the problems, Lynn getting sick at the last minute. I can't believe that of all people, *you* came through for me. Look at us. A month ago we didn't even know each other. And now—"

"It doesn't have to be over for us," Jann ventured.

"I'm so tired I can't think. Right now I just want to go to bed."

"That's a great idea. Let's—"

"Alone," she clarified.

He grinned. "I know. I was just going to suggest you forget everything tonight and rest. We'll see how you feel in the morning."

Jann placed his hand on the doorknob.

"Where are you going?" she asked

"I haven't gambled in quite a while. I thought I might try my hand at blackjack or something. See how I do."

In the morning, they packed in silence. The drapes were pulled wide open, exposing a serene desert panorama, bathing the room in a soft morning light. Tracey expected the tow truck any time.

"I didn't hear you come in last night?" she said.

"I didn't want to wake you."

"Did you win anything?"

"I did," Jann said. "I was doing so well I thought about staying another day but changed my mind. The room wouldn't be the same without you." *And neither will I.*

Tracey sadly acknowledged to herself she had probably let him down last night. He practically proposed and she wouldn't even consider it. *What an idiot!*

Jann zipped his bag closed about the time a knock sounded on the door.

"That must be the bellboy," Tracey said. She opened the door slightly and peered out.

"Torque! What are you—"

"Hi there, li'l lady. I heard there was some kind o' party goin' on."

"Well—yes."

"Mind if I join ya?"

She flung her arms around the old man and he cackled as she hugged him. "Of course, Torque. Come in."

As Torque removed his hat, Tracey realized he was wearing new clothes and a new hat.

"You're all dressed up? Where's old Buzzard Gut?"

"I couldn't come here lookin' like I hadn't seen a city in the last hunnerd years, so I made a trip down to Ro-Day-O Drive."

"You didn't?"

"Shore 'nuff did."

"Did they clean it?"

"No. But they was real nice. That dimestore cowboy behind the counter took one look at my hat and offered me five thousand dollars on the spot."

"You sold Buzzard Gut?" Tracey queried.

"No sir. I told him he could borrow it for a fee. Said

he'd put it in a glass case and take real good care of it 'til I wanted it back. Got a lawyer an' ever'thing.''

Tracey and Jann laughed.

''He told me it was the oldest Stetson in existence.''

''It probably is at that,'' Tracey agreed. ''Worth a fortune, too.''

''So—here I am. When's the weddin'?''

Torque's eyes glittered as they made connection with Jann's. Tracey turned to see Jann sheepishly shifting the strap of his bag over his shoulder.

''Uh-h-h—'' Jann hedged.

''Ya asked her, didn't ya, Jann?''

''Well, I—''

''Oh, no,'' Torque's voice quavered. ''Looks like I did it this time.''

''What's going on here, you two?'' Tracey demanded.

Torque swaggered past her, puffing his chest out as he crossed the room to inspect the view from their window. ''Ya see, I was told by Jann, over here, to hustle the tow truck over to Lost Wages first thing in the morning and deliver that Ferrari of his. Seems as if I have a Jaguar to tow and he's driving you back to L.A.'' Torque raised his feathered eyebrow. ''That *was* the message, wasn't it, Jann?''

Jann nodded.

''You *canceled* the tow *and* the car?'' Tracey confronted Jann with hands planted on her hips. ''Without talking to me?''

''He also said I better come cleaned up so's I could be his best man.''

Tracey gasped in stunned disbelief. ''That was rather presumptuous of you, Erikson.''

''I told you I hadn't gambled in a while—''

With both hands extended, Torque wedged himself between the two like a referee.

"Now don't get your fanny on fire, Tracey. Jann was just lookin' out for you."

"How's that?"

"They probably wouldn't know how to tow one of them foreign jobs," Torque explained. "It's *British,* y'know."

"And furthermore . . ." Tracey began.

Torque sidestepped nervously around Tracey, hopping from one foot to the other. "If you two will excuse me, I've got a sick Jaguar to load up. I can't be away from home too long—the church ladies, y'know."

Torque dipped his new hat at Tracey and edged around her as he made his way to the door. "I'll see you downstairs, Jann."

"How could you tell that sweet little old man we were getting married? You didn't really ask me. We haven't talked about this at all."

"I've known how I felt about you since the first day I saw you broken down on the side of the road."

"Jann," Tracey said, shaking her head, "that only happens in fairy tales. You can't base a relationship on how a person looks."

In a blur of motion, Jann set his bag down and gathered her into his strong arms. "I knew it then and I know it now. What about that little Love Chapel down the street? You might not be convinced we belong together, but I am."

Tracey leaned into his arms and raised a smiling face. "We do make a pretty good team, don't we?"

He kissed her deeply, slowly. "I've come to the same conclusion you have," he murmured. "I think we make a purrrrrrfect team."